Also by Teresa Milbrodt

Novel
The Patron Saint of Unattractive People

Short Story Collections
Bearded Women
Work Opportunities
Larissa Takes Flight

Instances of Head-Switching

Instances of Head-Switching

Teresa Milbrodt

Shade Mountain Press
Albany, New York

Shade Mountain Press
P.O. Box 11393
Albany, NY 12211
www.shademountainpress.com

Publisher's Cataloging-in-Publication data
Names: Milbrodt, Teresa, author.
Title: Instances of head-switching / Teresa Milbrodt
Description: First trade paperback original edition. | Albany, NY: Shade
    Mountain Press, 2020.
Identifiers: LCCN 2019949759 | ISBN 978-0-9984634-5-2 (paperback) | ISBN
    978-0-9984634-6-9 (ebook)
Subjects: LCSH: Magic realism (Literature). | People with disabilities—
    Fiction. | Goddesses—Fiction. | Monsters—Fiction. | Mythology—
    Fiction. | BISAC: FICTION / Magical Realism. | FICTION / Short Stories
    (single author).

Printed in the United States of America by Spencer Printing
10 9 8 7 6 5 4 3 2 1

Book design by Robin Parks.
Cover design by Whitney Pearce.
Cover art: *Negative Capability* by M.M. Dupay, © 2006 by M.M. Dupay,
mmdupay.com.

Shade Mountain Press publishes literature by women authors, especially women
from marginalized groups (women of color, LGBTQ women, women from
working-class backgrounds, disabled women). We aim to make the literary
landscape more diverse and more truly representative of the nation's artistic
voices.

Shade Mountain Press is a sponsored project of Fractured Atlas, a nonprofit arts
service organization. The work of Shade Mountain Press is made possible in
part by the New York State Council on the Arts with the support of Governor
Andrew M. Cuomo and the New York State Legislature.

For my mother, who never lost her sense of play,
and understands the importance of head-switching

Contents

The Monsters' War

AFTER THE war, when the monsters retreated, the four of us found apartments next door to each other. There was minimal damage to the complex compared to other buildings in town—some scraped paint and floor tile, no blood. There was nothing inside, no belongings or hints of the previous owners, and that was okay. We could find furniture. We wanted to start clean.

Marcus kissed the back of my neck in the morning to signal he was awake, but we didn't talk until he had his hearing aids in. Sometimes he wanted the world to be quiet for a while. There was always construction outside, or demolition, and I envied his ability to shut it out. Sometimes I missed the quiet of the cave where we'd lived for a month and a half. The glasses I had after the war weren't as good as my glasses before the war, and sometimes I left them off until I had to go to work. There wasn't much outside that I wanted to see clearly, at least not first thing in the morning.

After we'd decided it was safe to come back to town—following two weeks of reconnaissance—it took a while to account for things, like family and friends and jobs. Marcus lost both of his parents. They didn't die in the war, they weren't killed by monsters, but they suffered from the shortages. Both of them were in their late sixties but rather frail—his mom had kidney problems, his dad was diabetic, they needed medications. Maybe an infection took them, or the heat, but they lived far south of us where there was no electricity or clean water for weeks. It could have been anything that did it, but they shouldn't have died.

The monsters killed many through lack. They ate everything—power lines, sanitation plants, grocery stories, whole city blocks—and destroyed the rest. We heard things had been worse in other towns. Their monsters were larger, folks had to hide for longer periods of time with no canned soup or dried food packets, while the army fought what I imagined were sharp-toothed herds.

The government was stable and had new people in charge, but the nightly news recited ongoing construction projects that attested to what had happened. I knew plenty about construction since my office oversaw budgets and development plans. I spent all day erecting piles of numbers, knew it was good to rebuild, yet those projects marked by red pins on our wall maps were where the monsters had knocked over apartment buildings and swallowed families.

Some of my coworkers murmured that the monsters had come because of the government's broken promises to help poor people. There had been protests, riots, crowds on the verge of violent desperation when the government decided to tear down tent cities. Some said that social chaos always brought on monsters, conjuring them from the energy of unrest, and that's why they destroyed government buildings first. Everything else in town just got in the way.

OUR NEIGHBOR QUINN was a left-foot amputee, and his roommate Jones wore special shoes since one leg was shorter than the other. They'd known and liked each other before the war, but never said as much. Mostly they chatted in the laundry room because anything else would have been…strange. But living in that cave brought them together quite literally since we were sharing scratchy blankets, and then it wasn't hard to transition to sharing an apartment. That was good after we found out Quinn's younger sister had been killed. She lived in a town to our west, where the monsters had been larger and stayed longer. The apartment walls were thin, so we heard Quinn crying and swearing and Jones comforting him. I imagined them, arms around each other as they had been in the cave, though now they were perched on a secondhand couch, rocking back and forth.

Marcus said that even when you knew you were safe, you felt less so knowing that the monsters had killed your family, even if it was through shortages. That made it easier to think they could come back. But Marcus wanted to watch the nightly news, turned on the TV and used closed captioning so I didn't have to listen. I took off my glasses, blurring the world.

BEFORE THE WAR we four had not despised or supported the government. We supported staying alive. Some neighbors who stayed to fight the monsters gave us canned food and said to get out. I don't know what happened to them, only that they were trying to recruit people to stage a resistance, but with my vision and Marcus's hearing and Quinn's and Jones's slower gait, none of us were candidates.

We'd been living in the same apartment complex for years, didn't think of ourselves as left behind but banded together. Jones had camping gear, and I had two extra sleeping bags and the good flashlight. Quinn heard it was more peaceful to the north, so we could try to run or walk or limp there, but the rest of us didn't know what to think of the rumors.

"We can only know what's happening here," Marcus said on the night we clustered in the laundry room, wondering if it could serve as a bunker and deciding not. The best option was to hide. I don't want to say we escaped town, but when we left, stores were being looted, and there were rumors that monsters were on the horizon, along with strange lights.

The neighbors said that apartment buildings were being raided for spies and informants. Those who didn't like the government were suspected of aiding the monsters, though how that would happen I wasn't sure. We figured we wouldn't be targeted as monster collaborators, which was a relief and disappointing. Marcus and I liked the idea of being spies.

Jones knew the park north of town, had hiked many square miles and camped there several times. He'd found the cave, which he was almost positive didn't have prior inhabitants. With visions of monsters on our heels and sleeping bags on our backs, we forged through the trees. Marcus lost his hearing aids in the branches—they had an over-the-ear loop and must have snagged on something—so he could only hear sounds in a low register. I didn't have my good glasses, but he took my elbow and guided me over rocks, and I touched his shoulder when I heard noises that didn't seem to be us. We made out okay.

ONE OF MY coworkers had stayed in town to defend her apartment and see what happened.

"It got pretty chaotic," she said. "But the devils got what was coming to them."

She didn't mean the monsters, she meant the government. A number of people at my new job were darkly pleased that those stately buildings had been demolished by monsters. The enemy of my enemy might not be so bad.

Marcus hated people like that. "If you didn't fight the monsters, you might as well have been supporting murder," he said. I thought it was more complicated, but didn't try to argue the point.

My coworker, like others who stayed, had dealt with monsters before. She told me this rather proudly, showing that she'd lost two fingers. She didn't explain how, only that the government had taken her parents' land seven years ago to build a highway, or because they thought there was ore under the soil, or both. It was in the north of our state, and I'd heard so many stories about land seizures there that I got them mixed up. The government sent a bulldozer to tear down her parents' house. Her father cried. Her mother cursed and held him. He'd built the house forty years earlier. It was like ripping down a child. She said there was an invasion of monsters shortly after—not enough to make national news, but they ravaged a few bulldozers and dump trucks and delayed the government's project for a few months. Her parents moved to a small farmhouse that was in need of eternal fixing. They were still there. The monsters didn't tend to strike very rural areas.

My coworker brought muffins to work sometimes, blueberry or lemon poppyseed. Some people didn't eat them, some did, and others asked aloud where she'd gotten the blueberries and lemons since there weren't any in stores, just the black market. That hidden economy was mostly controlled by those who'd hated the former government, or so everyone said. I ate the muffins because my coworker was a good baker, and we worked together in the city under construction.

Everyone had different stories of monsters. In times like ours, what else were you supposed to do but explain your monsters to other people? Some days they were all we talked about when we had a coffee break. Other days we found different things to discuss, like friends who had just returned to town and were looking for work or new apartments, or how there was starting to be more fresh produce in stores.

I knew some people would never come back. They were living with family, or had found new jobs elsewhere, or didn't have the resources to return, or simply knew that larger cities like ours were more vulnerable to attack.

Some of my coworkers said they were sure the monsters had retreated for a long time. I no longer used words like "sure" and "certain."

WHEN WE LEFT town it was the middle of the night. Quinn and Jones decided I should have the gun because my vision was so bad without my glasses, which I hadn't been able to find while I was stuffing clothes and dry soup packets into a duffel bag. I hadn't shot much before, but Quinn declared my aim good enough for our escape. He said he'd tell people that I was blind, and I had the gun. I protested since I could still see color and movement without my glasses, but Quinn said blindness was better. I could

5

"sight" people by listening to their footfalls, and I wouldn't feel guilty if I had to kill anyone since I wouldn't see them go down. I said I would too see them go down and I would probably feel awful. Quinn said the story was better, since it would freak people out. I carried the gun.

Six weeks later when we returned to town, Marcus ordered new hearing aids. It took three weeks for them to arrive since all the mail and delivery services had been interrupted. My new glasses prescription gave me a headache by the end of the day, but it was better than nothing. Without them my astigmatism was so bad that I saw everything shadowed. When looking at people from a distance, they seemed to be walking around with a ghost self.

My parents had weathered the monsters. They lived in a small cabin near a lake, four hours south of the city. They had a gas stove, a small generator, a steady supply of fish since my mother had become an avid fisherwoman in her retirement, and Dad has adopted a love of gardening and canning. They were pleased with their self-sufficiency, which had come in handy during times of monsters. They had not yet met Marcus, but called as soon as phone lines had been repaired since they had worried over me for weeks. I told them of our camping odyssey, and that I was living with Marcus. They said to give him their love and condolences, and they would try to visit soon. Too many roads were still under construction to make the drive.

I was almost embarrassed to tell Marcus my parents were fine, mumbled the news while we were making dinner. He made me repeat myself three times until he understood, then he hugged me tight, a ladle still in his hands, and whispered, "Good. We don't need any more losses."

JONES AND QUINN returned to work when the schools reopened. They were both teachers. Jones taught second grade, and Quinn taught high school chemistry. They said the kids were happy to get back to a routine that felt normal, though they had new classmates and things were kind of crowded since some of the school buildings had been destroyed. But Jones told me quietly that a bunch of his students were coming to school bleary-eyed. Maybe they were having nightmares. Maybe they weren't living in the best of places. After lunch he had them write or draw stories, which meant he saw their monsters towering over houses, devouring apartments. They had the bodies of lions or dragons, with scorpion tails. In one of the pictures, a kid was cutting the monster's stomach open with scissors so everything could come out—his house and parents and the corner store.

I knew monsters were still eating Marcus's dreams. Often I woke to him holding me tightly, his arms too rigid for sleep. He had a new job with city planning and infrastructure, spent his days studying everything below the pavement, the maze of pipes and drains and sewers, which someone had to know to approve of the new construction projects I was helping to build with numbers. I wondered if he thought monsters, small ones, could be hiding in those pipes, biding their time.

I didn't want to say I'd forgotten anything—the loss of a good job, several friends, a great secondhand couch, my grandmother's jewelry, and a sense of security that someone wouldn't wake me in the middle of the night and say I had to get out. Now. But I tried to allow for moments when the past year didn't echo through my mind. I didn't think Marcus had been able to do that, and quietly assumed he was slipping out of bed and spending nights tracking monsters through the underground networks of the city. But the monsters had taken his parents. How could he not feel that loss in every heartbeat?

THERE WERE MANY stories about what the monsters looked like, and everyone saw them differently—when they arrived, when they left, whether they were still lingering in shadows. Some people thought they had whip-like tails, others gave them scales or fur. My coworker's monsters were different from mine—yellow and gargantuan and appearing in daylight with terrible claws, while my monsters came at night with feet that made the pavement tremble, but they could shrink to the size of a small dog when

7

they wanted to hide. In the end it didn't matter what they looked like, because we all agreed on the destruction they had caused, the people they had killed, the tears left in our illusion of security.

Most of my stories were from the six weeks in that cave. I did not tell them at the bar. After Marcus and I had made love for the sixth time, we were lying near the mouth of the cave wrapped in a sleeping bag and scratchy camp blanket. *Why is everything that's supposed to be warm so damn uncomfortable?* I wondered to myself but didn't say to Marcus because I would have had to yell. I heard the rustle of monsters in the leaves, or rather I heard the rustle and put my finger to Marcus's lips, pointing outside. I was sure if we made noise the monster would find us and laugh, two pitiful naked creatures trying to find desire in the mouth of war, then it would consume us as it had eaten so many other people.

Marcus and I held each other and wormed our way back, scrunching into darkness. I listened, feeling his eyes on me, waiting for a signal that we would be okay, that the monsters had passed, though I wasn't sure when I could give it. Jones and Quinn were asleep, but they'd reported hearing rustlings outside before. Monsters on patrol? It was mostly safe in the forest with our gun, but there was no certainty.

Later I wondered what my coworker was doing in town at that moment. When it came to wars and monsters, you had to remember that there were many stories bumping around like bubbles, and they were all happening while you tried to avoid the one small monster that wanted to swallow your life. In that moment it was allowed to be impossibly large and eclipse everything else. In later weeks and months and years, it was allowed to give you insomnia.

THE MONSTERS WERE greedy and gluttonous; on that we agreed. They killed parents, so there were many children who needed new ones. Families reconfigured out of love and necessity. My coworker was caring for two nephews who'd lived in a town to the south. She didn't say what had happened to their parents, just that the little one was five years old and cried for his mother every night.

I gave her a plate of chocolate chip cookies for them, a recipe I remembered from before the war since I'd made it so many times. It was good to bake in my new kitchen, and Marcus had found chocolate chips at the store at five in the morning when he went to shop because he couldn't sleep. That was the secret to pouncing on rare goods that sold out quickly.

"Thank you," said my coworker, bringer of black market blueberry muffins, since that form of exchange existed for those who were not early birds. I'd tell Marcus I shared the cookies with coworkers, but not with whom. On my walk home I wondered if larger allegiances, even political ones, could be born out of small friendships and baked goods, or if that would just save a few people who'd otherwise perish the next time monsters came to town. But I couldn't ask those questions, because after I gave her the cookies she smiled like she was glad I was alive now, and I smiled to return the sentiment, the small allegiance that would work for now.

SO WHERE IS my heart? I figure pieces of it have been shearing off over the past year. It is in the linoleum of my old apartment that is no more, lying in rubble surrounded by glass shards. It is in the cave where Marcus and I started holding hands when it was too dangerous to build a fire because of the smoke. It is tucked into corners around my desk at my new job, and it is hiding under our bed and keeping watch for monsters. It is in our kitchen beside the sugar bin. You should not keep your heart all in one place. I would like to think that is a lesson I learned over the past few months, but maybe I knew it already.

And what have I learned? That I should give cookies to other people who were plagued by monsters? That I should stay quiet after making love because you never know what might happen? That I should tell my boyfriend kind lies? Where is the knowledge I want to have found? Does it exist? It seems I should have gained something, but that's the piece I'm still wanting, waiting for, and if I lie very quietly beside my restless Marcus, listening to his non-dreams, maybe it will come to me.

Marbles

THEY WERE ALL different colors. I called them marbles because that's what they looked like, marbles or gumballs, neatly arranged in a plastic container with a small compartment for each one. If anyone had walked into my room, they would have thought it was a large pill box.

I mixed and matched the marbles depending on my work schedule. Sometimes I had to take pride (light blue) and forget about humble (peach). Other days it was better to have assertiveness (light pink) but not aggression (crimson), and extra kindness (spring green) and compassion (lavender). Even jealousy (indigo) was useful in certain situations. It added to my drive, and I didn't feel so bad about repossessing a huge flat-screen TV that was much nicer than anything I could afford. It wasn't a good marble to swallow every day and regurgitate at night since it caused a slight burning sensation in my esophagus, but I don't know how I could have survived the repo side of the rent-to-own business if it weren't for the marbles.

I was a small woman, not the sort of person you could imagine confiscating computers, but I had my own bills to pay and I was quite good at the job. Not everyone can leave bits of their personality at home, and frankly some people—the unrepentant and repeat offenders—didn't deserve my compassion. They had to say goodbye to that stereo after six months of unpaid bills.

I could heft eighty pounds, which most people didn't expect. Weekends at the gym and days at my job helped to develop my biceps. People didn't always take me seriously when I asked for the TV. They crossed their arms and told me to just try it. When I succeeded in hauling out the wide-screen or La-Z-Boy on my dolly, they screamed and called me a bitch.

That hurt a bit, even if I was being called a bitch by someone who'd made endless promises to give us the money "next month." Often I swallowed the callous (slate gray) and indifferent (pea green) marbles, so insults slid right off me. I kept a plastic pill bottle in my car since I needed a place to spit a couple of the harsher marbles when I was on my lunch break. I didn't want to be unnecessarily short with the poor girl working the drive-though. Usually I kept the compassion marble in my bottle, just in case it was needed. Sometimes kids cried when the TV was taken away, and I couldn't shrug and say "Tough."

My boss said I was the best repo person he'd ever hired. I knew the burnout rate was high. When I went in for the interview he was skeptical, but I had anticipated this and swallowed the personality of a CEO—no-nonsense and confrontational, with extra determination (bright orange) and fortitude (fire engine red).

"Sir, if you don't think I can handle the position, let me know and I'll look somewhere else." My voice was cold enough to freeze water. I folded my hands on his desk, leaned over, and gave him a smile that was more calculating than friendly. He nodded and said I had the job, figuring I'd last a week, but I'd stayed on for five years.

I INHERITED THE marbles from my grandma, who had been an emergency room nurse for thirty-five years. She didn't talk about her time at the hospital other than to say those decades had been rather eventful, and the marbles helped.

"These things tend to skip a generation," she told me without further comment on why she didn't give the marbles to my mom instead. The best I could figure was that Grandma needed them until she retired. I was ten when she decided I was ready to start swallowing them. You had to do that when you were young for the marbles to be truly effective.

"And keep it to yourself," she told me every time we practiced the circus art of regurgitation. I was the oldest grandchild, a sometimes overly sensitive kid, so I knew the marbles' potential value. Grandma gave them to me for keeps when I was fifteen and she moved to Arizona. She said high school was a good time to be in control of your emotions. When my mother wondered aloud why I wasn't a teen drama queen, I shrugged and smiled and went back to my room to spit up tranquility.

I DIDN'T HAVE a boyfriend, I had Geoff, who was a friend with benefits. The arrangement worked well because I was so tired by the end of the week that I didn't have time for romance. I wanted a good cuddle with no strings attached. Geoff worked at a bank and put in sixty-hour weeks that he hoped would help him climb the corporate ladder. He didn't want to live with someone else and risk alienating them with his crazy schedule. We were perfect for each other.

Every Friday night he came over to my apartment. We ate pizza and ice cream, bitched about our jobs, and then screwed. It was excellent therapy for us both, and helped me unwind even better than the tranquility (cream) marble. The sexy (violet) and sympathetic (forest green) marbles were good for date nights. Geoff was growing a bit of a paunch even though he was in his late thirties, and he was very self-conscious about it.

"I know I need to go to the gym," he said, "and I've been eating too much fast food, but I don't have time for anything else."

"I think it's cute," I said, being perfectly honest because I was sympathetic. Then I told him to fuck me because I was feeling sexy. This was also good for his self-confidence.

When Geoff wasn't around—which was most nights—I regurgitated my marbles after dinner. It was nice to ignore my phone and calmly watch TV. I kept the tranquility marble rolling around in my stomach so my mind didn't feel too blank.

Whenever I spoke with my grandma after her move to Arizona and a marble-less life, she'd always been calm and Zen.

"I don't know how she does it," my mother said.

I didn't know how she did it without feeling a deep and disturbing void, but Grandma told me that after a lifetime of marbles she was ready for a break.

"I can touch a memory and let it go," she said like they were nothing but butterflies flitting past her head. I couldn't think about that right now because I still needed the marbles. Badly.

I LIKED THE other repo guys for the most part and worked with them on occasion. Skip and Jack were cool and efficient and never said much except "We've come for the couch." Most guys did the job and left fast, except for Melvin who was kind of sadistic and seemed to take extra time packing up confiscated items. He made me shiver if I'd swallowed the compassion marble that day. Melvin called the customers poor saps and said they got what they deserved.

Many of our customers were not poor saps, they were honest and well-meaning and just didn't have much money. Others were assholes, but I could tell one from the other pretty quick and gauge the situation accordingly. My boss wanted to negotiate whenever possible, see if we could find a deal, and half the time it worked. Often they just needed someone to listen. Like the young wife whose husband had been laid off. The single guy raising three kids and working two jobs who still couldn't afford a couch and two laptops. The elderly woman who depended on her television for news and company. I had to listen to their struggles but not be duped. It was a delicate balance, especially since the wrong combinations of marbles had side effects like an adverse drug reaction.

I was on my third deal with Leslie, a single mother who worked ten-hour days in a nursing home and needed the television to give her son company when he came home from school. When my boss sent me back to her apartment a fourth time I started to wonder how nice we could be, but with the compassion marble rolling around in my stomach, I had to nod and listen to her story about how they had cut her hours at work from fifty to forty a week and she didn't know how she would get by.

"We'll manage, I hope," she said, brushing a hair out of her eye. She had changed out of her nursing home scrubs to jeans and a T-shirt with a rubber duck on it. Leslie seemed sweet and somewhat frazzled, but her apartment was clean and her kid's hair was brushed. Given her work schedule, those were notable accomplishments that suggested she was responsible. I kept in mind that she was younger than me and had more financial duties, a child to support and no one else helping out.

"I'll see what we can do for you," I said.

"Thank you," she said, grinning and touching my arm like I was an older sister.

When I got back into my car I wondered if my boss would agree to a fourth deal. That was starting to push things a bit, but I could make him consent. I had to for her sake. I spit out the compassion marble.

Sometimes I wondered if anything I felt was authentic, but in the end I decided that yes, the emotions were real. They were my marbles to swallow or not as I chose, and everyone had to shut off pieces of themselves from time to time. It was just a little easier for me.

THE DAY I couldn't find the compassion marble I freaked out. I was ready to call in sick, but I knew it was going to be a full week. My boss needed me, so I racked my brain for substitute marbles, and went with sympathy. That made it harder to take stuff back. More than once I stood in the doorway to some modest trailer home, TV or laptop in my arms, and dammit, I almost couldn't walk forward. I was feeling too bad for the poor customers, who were obviously scraping to get by. But I had to clench my stomach around the assertive marble and march toward my van.

At home that evening I experimented with different marble combinations. It was better to do that on the weekend when it didn't matter who I interacted with, but this was an emergency. Sympathy and jealousy—an odd combination—proved to be the most effective, but it also gave me nasty diarrhea. While I didn't digest the marbles it was clear they affected my digestive system, like any strong emotion might do. I didn't feel like eating much but cereal and toast, and I was never more relieved than when I found the compassion marble on Saturday. I'd spit it out in my vitamin pill box by mistake, left it on the kitchen table, and didn't think to look there until I was refilling my weekly supplements.

GEOFF SAID HE could be relaxed and honest around me in a way he couldn't with other people. I was relaxed around him, too, and honest about everything but the marbles.

"Do you ever think about getting married?" Geoff asked me after we'd polished off a medium pepperoni pizza and a pint of mint chocolate chip ice cream.

"Sometimes, but not really," I said. The marbles would complicate relationships. With the contentment marble rolling around my gut, I could be happy with my own company.

Geoff was quiet. My sympathy marble kicked in.

"Do you think about getting married?" I asked.

"I think about it, but I'm not sure," he said, gazing at my ceiling. "Some nights I get home and I can't stand to be around people. I'd probably scream at a family if I had one."

I slid my arm around his shoulders. "It's rough."

He kissed my cheek. "You're sweet."

I wondered if the friends-with-benefits relationship was turning into something else, or if Geoff was at least considering that possibility. I'd never tried the love (deep pink) marble with him for obvious reasons. We were about camaraderie and bodily comfort, and that was it. I'd only used that particular marble a few times, like when I found three mangy puppies two blocks from my apartment building. They were flea-bitten and pitiful, smelled badly, and didn't even have a cardboard box for shelter.

I knew they needed mothering, so I whisked them home and dumped them in the bathtub, then swallowed the love marble while they were mewling. I washed the dirt from their fur, brushed them best I could, and took them to the Humane Society. I couldn't have pets in my apartment, but after giving up those poor puppies I sat crying in the car until I spit out the love marble. It was powerful stuff, but love and jealously were the most potent marbles. Sometimes I considered flushing those two down the toilet, but I stopped myself in time. I needed the complete set.

Were there times when I didn't want to swallow a marble? Of course. Did I do it anyway? Of course. Was I happy about it when all was said and done? Usually. But most of those occasions were related to work. Love was optional.

I WAS ABLE to negotiate a fourth deal for Leslie, and frankly I was quite pleased about that, but then I had to return the next month because she hadn't made the regular payment, or the extra ten dollars she'd promised to kick in. As usual she had a story.

"Sammy and I went to visit my mom for her birthday," she told me from the stove where she was stirring pasta sauce. Today she was wearing jeans and a lilac T-shirt, somehow immaculate despite the red sauce, though her hair was coming out of her bun in wisps. "Then we broke down and had to call for a tow. It turned out that the car needed a transmission rebuild. Do you know how much those things cost?"

I shook my head because I did not know about transmissions, just TVs. Compassion dictated that I believe her, and I wanted to believe her because all of the hard-luck stories sounded reasonable. Shit happened, often on a regular basis, often when you didn't have much money, and what was I supposed to do, ask for the receipts? Probably. But I didn't want to embarrass her, or myself, with prying questions. I told her I'd see what we could do.

"You're such a sweetheart," she said from beside the stove, trying to stir the pasta water and sauce and keep an eye on the garlic bread in the oven. Logic intervened as I walked back to my car. She had to be paying the cable bill, so why not us? We were too soft. I was too soft. Or was it that the rest of the world was lacking in compassion?

My boss raised an eyebrow at the latest agreement, but I had swallowed my confidence marble along with compassion and assured him things would work out for her in two weeks, by the time of her next paycheck. I imagined Leslie sitting at her kitchen table, still in that lilac T-shirt, and writing out a long-overdue check. For a moment I felt like I'd swallowed a clairvoyance marble, then I started thinking that a clairvoyance marble was a good idea. I was always coming up with new marbles I needed, and I wondered if my grandma had felt the same way. There were so many questions I wanted to ask her. Why hadn't I thought of these things while she was still alive and I wasn't the only person in the world who understood what it felt like to be me?

SOME NIGHTS I admit I got lonely. Geoff was kind and brought me chocolate bars with caramel and said he looked forward to our evenings together. I did, too. Geoff had a good sense of humor, and I liked his thoughtfulness. He considered things carefully before speaking, unlike most of the people I worked with.

It was good to mix up my marbles, and not swallow the same set day after day. When I didn't vary the routine, I started to feel weird, and it was harder to spit the marbles out at night. I wondered if a little more love would be good for me, and decided to try it with Geoff the following Friday night, just to see how my body reacted.

It was not good to swallow love before pizza, since we were talking and laughing and eating and I saw something in Geoff's eyes that I hadn't seen before, an affection I couldn't quite name, and then I wondered if I was looking at him in the same way. His feet grazed mine under the table. My stomach and heart and brain lurched.

After dinner I had to excuse myself, go to the bathroom, disgorge the marble, and throw up. I rinsed out my mouth to rid it of the sour taste of pizza and stomach acid, and cupped the pink marble in my palm. Geoff and I were both nearing forty. We liked each other. We were wondering about our futures. I knew people who said that when they were in love it was so fantastic and overwhelming it made them want to vomit. Though my reaction wasn't out of the ordinary, I wasn't sure I wanted to put up with it.

"Are you okay?" Geoff asked me when I came out of the bathroom.

"Just fine," I said, but I didn't want ice cream. I hid the love marble in my vitamin box on the kitchen table while Geoff was queuing up the movie on my TV. When I sat back on the couch he rested his arm around my shoulders.

"You're sure you're okay?" he said.

"Sure I'm sure," I said and kissed him on the cheek. The compassion marble was doing its thing, and I didn't want him to be uncomfortable.

But I thought about the love marble during our after-movie fuck, which I wasn't really excited about but had to do to prove to Geoff that I was fine. Damn compassion anyway. Part of me wondered what would have happened if I'd swallowed the love marble before fucking. But I was scared to try it.

I spent the next week pondering my marbles. They enabled me to do my job. My boss needed someone who could be tactful. Our customers needed someone who wasn't heartless. At night I had to spit out compassion and swallow tranquility because compassion gave me a headache. I thought about our customers too much, how I'd become familiar with them and their stories over the years. They were often one paycheck away from broke, and needed someone to cut them slack for a month or two. Dwelling on them was easy since I lived alone. But if I lived with someone else, that might create more complications. I'd never seen Geoff angry, and I didn't want to confront frustrated or sad at home. I saw enough of that at work, and it was exhausting. Not even the marbles could make me feel less weary after a long day.

THAT FRIDAY GEOFF told me how his boss had bawled him out for some stupid little mistake at work like he was a trainee instead of a twelve-year employee. Somehow that criticism ignited his fears over losing hair and going gray and gaining weight.

"It's stupid to get worked up about aging," he sighed. "It happens to everyone." He kissed my forehead and slid his arm behind my shoulders as we reclined on the couch. My fingers ached with something I hoped was not a twinge of arthritis. We weren't old but we weren't young and we didn't mind seeing each other naked with the lights on. I wondered how many other opportunities I'd have to find this kind of relationship, one that was relaxed and congenial and not based on trying to romance or impress the hell out of each other.

I did one more test to see how it felt to have the love marble rolling around in my system when Geoff wasn't around. I swallowed it on Monday morning, but then I couldn't stop thinking about Geoff or remember which house I was supposed to go to next. I spit the marble out at lunch to clear my head. This wasn't good. Would there ever be the right emotional cocktail? I started feeling despair and spat out all the marbles—six of them—since I wasn't sure which one was causing the adverse reaction. I wanted to sit in my car and feel blank, erasing everything from my mind so all that remained was cold logic.

How did everyone else manage the ebb and flow of emotions, the marbles rolling around in their own heads and stomachs, and would it have been better for me if I'd remained the sweet and somewhat overly sensitive kid who worried all evening over whether she'd said the right things at school?

When I called Leslie again to ask why she hadn't paid this month's rental fee plus fifteen bucks, she explained that she had been sick and her son had been sick and she missed four days of work and maybe I should come over to see what we could work out. I hung up my cell phone and texted Skip, asking if he could get this one because I was pretty busy, but Leslie was a polite lady and had a nice kid. He texted back and said sure, no problem, he understood. I tried not to feel sick. At least I hadn't sent Melvin.

I WONDERED WHAT it would be like to swallow all my marbles at once and never spit them out. I wondered what it would be like to go without them for one day. Maybe I needed to do something with the love marble so it couldn't be an easy temptation. Freeze it in an ice cube tray so it had to melt before it would take effect. Lock it in a safety deposit box at the bank so I'd have to drive there to retrieve it. Seal it in a little box at the bottom of a much larger box full of books far back in my closet. Anything to give me more time to consider the swallow.

I was resolute about that decision until the next time I saw Geoff. We had pizza and chocolate ice cream with chocolate chunks in it, which may have had something to do with what came next.

"I love you," said Geoff as we snuggled on the couch, full and sleepy. The words shot me bright awake. I closed my eyes for a moment, kissed his forehead, and considered my response. Could I lie convincingly without the love marble in my gut?

"I love you, too," I said, though it was the compassion marble talking, and I knew that was what he needed to hear. I swallowed hard to keep all the marbles down. Could I love Geoff? I closed my eyes. Maybe tomorrow or the next day I could swallow the love marble again and see what happened. There would be side effects—a rise in blood pressure, indigestion, insomnia— but maybe they would dissipate with time. Maybe I could get used to them.

For the moment I shook my head, dislodging the question and leaning against his shoulder, focusing on the tranquility in my gut. But there was something odd. A fluttering lightness. A twinge of acid. Even when it persisted, I told myself it was just too much pizza and ice cream. Nothing more.

The Mirror

LATER I CALLED it a fight. He said it was an extended discussion conducted at high volume. We couldn't agree on much anymore.

This time we'd been yelling about whether or not it made sense for me to get a job. He said I should do volunteer work a few hours every week, perhaps knit scarves for orphans, but nothing too taxing. He liked coming home to a hot dinner and a tidy house.

"Housekeeping and daily chores take a lot of work," he said.

"Not so much that I don't have time for anything else," I said. "I don't want cooking and cleaning to be the focus of my life."

He bristled when I said that, like making sure we had a comfortable home should have been more than enough for me. Cooking and cleaning had been more than enough when I was still living with the dwarfs, but there were seven of them plus me, and the dwarfs were happy to do the dishes and scrub pots after supper. I didn't bring this up to him, though I considered it.

"We'll talk about this tomorrow," he said, which is when I threw the plate at him. We'd had this discussion before, several times actually, and "tomorrow" never came.

"You're impossible," he yelled before storming out the door, probably going down to the tavern for a pint.

I was still breathing heavily. "That felt good," I told the ghostly green face in the mirror.

It nodded sagely. "A little cathartic plate smashing can be good for the soul, but best not make it a habit."

"I know, I know," I sighed. But I didn't particularly like our dishes, anyway. They had gold edging, too fancy for my tastes. My husband had picked them out.

He didn't know about the mirror's face or past history, just that it hung in the living room. I'd inherited it after the death of my stepmother, though I didn't consult it for the same reasons she had. I knew I was pretty, and who cared if I was the prettiest in the land? I needed a therapist, not a beauty consultant, which is where the mirror came in. My husband never listened to me, making me wonder if he'd ever listened in the first place.

When we'd been king and queen, it hadn't mattered so much.

We'd been lucky to escape the castle with the mirror and our lives after the raid. As fiery arrows arced over the walls and a battering ram was rolled to the gate, we donned heavy gray cloaks and left through a secret entrance that dumped us into the woods. It had been a year and a half since we'd fled the kingdom, and he hadn't recovered from the insult of being shoved off the throne.

"I didn't spend enough money to equip the army," he lamented at dinner the next evening. I'd made bangers and mash, his new favorite supper, but even that didn't put him in a good mood when he was determined to be sore. Our subjects had liked him, so he'd assumed his reign was secure, but he hadn't counted on outside foes. "With a larger militia, we wouldn't have needed to flee."

I forked another bite of mashed potato and resisted the urge to shrug. We'd had to get new identities and a new cottage, but he'd never forget that he'd been a prince and then a king. I wished he could. He was much more stressed and less charming than he'd been when we were first married. My husband wanted to assume the usual man's role and take care of me, but I wanted to help care for us both.

"I could clean the homes of wealthy people," I said, but he balked at that.

"You were a queen," he said. "You can't lower yourself to tidying up after others."

I muttered that I'd cleaned up after seven dwarfs for a number of months and been just fine, thank you very much. He grimaced at his plate and asked for more sausages. I resisted the urge to tell him he could get them himself if he didn't want me serving other people.

I didn't mind life as a commoner, but after the plate incident I was surprised that breaking things felt as good as it did. I'd been sweet and mild-mannered before, like a *princess*, so it was satisfying to do something a little bad. As king he'd maintained a calm and friendly demeanor, taking jaunts around the kingdom on horseback to distribute bread and wave beneficently to peasants. But he didn't understand what it was like to live in the village and be a normal person. Now he had to figure that out, and I thought it was good for him. Educational.

But life was bad for those who still resided in our old kingdom. The new ruler was an awful tyrant, my mirror confirmed. I didn't tell my husband. He'd go crazy, try to raise an army, and probably get himself killed. It was far better for him to stay at his current job as a bookkeeper, since he was good with figures. Ten years of private tutoring had assured that.

I WAS AWFULLY bored with cooking and cleaning and doing laundry, which is why I asked the mirror to teach me a few of my stepmother's transformation spells. The mirror went into great detail, explaining spells I could use to make myself older or younger, or even the opposite gender. I tried the crone spell first, and found it was particularly amusing to see myself as a gray-haired old lady.

"Can't I be a little plumper?" I asked the mirror. "Plump old ladies are cute, and they look more trustworthy. The skinny ones look like they're up to something."

"As you wish," said the mirror, teaching me a few extra words to fill out my cheeks, waist, and bosom so I looked more like someone's kindly great-aunt. That was the guise I used to get a part-time job with a seamstress.

People figured that cute old ladies were good at things like sewing and doling out wisdom. The women who frequented the shop where I worked were all too willing to confide in me and ask for advice with their children, marriages, and aging parents.

"You're always so helpful, Auntie," they said, hugging my soft shoulders.

"Happy to help, my dears," I said, patting my gray curls.

The not-quite-a-crone spell was the best thing that had ever happened to me. No one was willing to spill their guts in front of me when I'd been queen. Then they had to be fake cheery, assuming I was pretty and clueless and didn't understand real people. But sometimes winning others' trust was based on how you looked, a sad fact I used to my advantage.

I turned into an old man when I wanted to have a beer and spy on my husband in the local tavern. I found him wet-eyed in front of his ale, bemoaning his situation to the bartender, who nodded while he polished a glass.

"My boss wants me to work faster," my husband groused. "I made two miscalculations in the books today, and when he found out I thought he'd give me a thrashing."

My husband wasn't accustomed to being yelled at. Before, he'd done the yelling. I sat at a table in the corner and watched him, pleased that he was telling his problems to *someone*, but upset that he put on a mask for me, his wife. I wanted to know these things, too.

I sipped my beer and shook my head. I'd survived three attempts on my life in the past, so certainly I could listen to my husband's problems without breaking down in tears. I took on another part-time job as a bookkeeper for the tavern so I could keep a curious eye on him and listen to his laments while doing figures. Maybe it was the fact that I'd been walking around as an old woman for a while, but I was starting to feel more maternal toward him. But he'd been trying to care for me ever since we'd moved, which was something I didn't particularly like.

Maybe we were better parents than lovers.

I was busier and happier than I'd ever been, and thought it was a shame that my stepmother hadn't used the mirror in more interesting ways. Being pretty was a pain. You had to waste all that energy on staying pretty, and that could make you strange and obsessive. It was much more fun to turn myself into someone who could have an interesting life.

THE MIRROR GAVE me sober updates on how the situation in the old kingdom was going from bad to worse. I pondered the problem while adjusting the hems on velvet dresses. For several afternoons in a row I daydreamed plots, wondering if I could return to the castle as my old-lady self, covertly spy on the new ruler, and see if there were any plans for a revolt.

I didn't want my husband back in power. He was a kind man, but I quietly enjoyed seeing his frustration in the evening, hearing him rant that he wasn't being paid enough for the work he did. He'd grown up in gilded rooms and never had to toil so hard or endure criticism.

But I loved my former kingdom and its inhabitants too much to let them suffer if I thought I could do something. My subjects were enduring the usual cruel tyranny—baseless arrests, imprisonment for anyone who spoke against the king, and all the pretty young girls were being recruited for jobs as ladies-in-waiting. At least that's what they were told.

When I launched my plan, I explained to my husband that I was going to visit my friends the dwarfs, as it had been forever since I'd seen them. Instead I shrouded myself in the old woman's skin and took a job in the castle kitchen. A month of kneading bread dough and listening closely to conversations was just enough to understand the new political machinations—who supported the regime and who was launching a resistance movement and trying to organize everyone else.

I attended meetings in darkened cottages, listened to their plans, and supplied detailed maps of the castle's hidden passages and secret rooms with extra ammunition.

"How did you ever come by these, Grandmother?" said Artin, one of the revolt's leaders.

"You'd be surprised what kind of information an old woman can glean if she keeps her ears open," I said, tapping the side of my head. No one doubted my honesty or my identity, and I relished the evenings spent with my former subjects. They were intelligent men and women, excellent storytellers, and didn't give themselves airs. They had the same work ethic as my dear dwarfs, whom I did need to visit at some point, but not until this crisis was resolved.

I loved Artin's children to bits, brought them toys and sweet buns and told them stories about a princess who just wanted to live like everyone else.

"Castle life gets boring," I explained. "You can't run around or make noise. You get to wear pretty dresses, but if one of them gets ripped in the garden, you get yelled at for an hour."

"You speak as though from experience, Grandmother," Artin's wife, Lela, teased me.

"No," I said, "just a good imagination."

I'd never had the opportunity to chat with my subjects like this. Now they weren't people under my rule. They were friends. After the children went to bed, Artin and I reviewed castle maps and I suggested the best ways for outside forces to enter.

"You're an angel and a general," Artin said. I blushed. My husband didn't know I'd read his books on military tactics in the library when I was bored. The more I thought about it, there were entirely too many sides of me he didn't know, but so many of them could emerge when I was freed of my young body and nestled into an older one.

The mirror had warned I needed to change back into a young woman nightly or risk the transformation spell becoming permanent. In my small cook's chambers, it wasn't hard to manage the metamorphosis and giggle a little behind my cupped hands. I hadn't thought fooling everyone would be so much fun. The strange thing was, after a few weeks, changing back into my younger self felt strange. Almost unnatural. It was how I'd looked when I'd been a princess and a queen and ultimately ignored by anyone who was making important decisions. As an old woman I (allegedly) had age and experience on my side.

ALL THIS MASQUERADING had made me hone my talents for concealment and stealth, so it was simple to hide a packet of poison in my apron pocket and slip a few grains in the soup and bread dough. When the new king slumped over at the dinner table, our attack began.

Even as arrows started to fly, I was calm and controlled, unafraid of dying in battle. My stepmother had tried to kill me many times, but now I'd taken hold of my fate. I was tempted to pick up a dagger—if I were killed it would be for a good reason—but I made myself duck out of the castle through the same passage I'd used when we had to flee the first time.

It was hard to leave the newly free kingdom, since I was more invested in it and its people than I'd been before. I couldn't forget Artin and his children and my other friends, but I had to return home to my husband, who still needed me. I had been gone for eight weeks, but hid the details of our insurrection and said I'd had a lovely time with the dwarfs.

"I missed you," my husband said, giving me a hug like he really meant it. I squeezed him back. Now that I was home I realized how much I'd missed him, too. I also understood more about his investment in the kingdom, even if I didn't think he'd really connected with its people. Neither had I, before now, but every day I found myself aching to return and see everyone.

I consulted the mirror daily for reports on the kingdom's new governing council. Artin was its leader, but his vote counted the same as everyone else's. They made some good decisions and some not-so-good ones in the rebuilding process. I wished I could join them and be an extra voice of caution. They needed to invest more money in fortifications and reconstruction, or risk another takeover, but I reassured myself daily that they had everything under control.

TWO MONTHS LATER, my husband heard about the uprising and formation of a new government. Of course he wanted to return to the old kingdom.

"Just imagine the parades they'll have in my honor," he said.

"I don't think they want a king again," I said.

"But they loved me," my husband said.

"I want to stay here," I said. "I got sick of all those satin and velvet dresses. I like our cottage and this village and I'm perfectly happy." I knew I wouldn't survive if I couldn't put on the skin of an old woman and go to the seamstress shop every day for the usual chatter.

My husband pouted for a day, then quit his bookkeeeper job and left without me. I found the note on the kitchen table when I returned from marketing. He said he would love for me to join him if I changed my mind. I made bangers and mash for dinner and sulked. I'd left the kingdom and returned for him, but he cared more about that stupid old crown than he did about me.

"Maybe we've grown too far apart," I sulked to the mirror.

"Or maybe your hearts are close to the same place," it said.

It took one more day before I broke down and started the journey back to our kingdom. I went as my old-lady self, though the mirror reminded me again that spending too long under any transformation spell meant it would stick. I was willing to accept the consequences.

When I arrived at Artin's cottage, the governing council was having a meeting. They'd declared his home to be their new headquarters until they could build a new town hall.

The discussion stopped when I arrived. All of the council members stood up and embraced me, saying, "Grandmother, we wondered where you'd gone." I claimed weakness, saying I'd needed to recuperate for some weeks since I was exhausted.

"You're welcome to join the meeting as an adviser on the council," Artin told me, then the council members resumed what they'd been doing when I entered.

Berating my husband. I assumed this had been going on for some time, as he had his hands folded in his lap and looked quite beaten down.

"Waltzing in here and telling us you should be king again," Artin said. "Have you no humility?"

"I still say we should tar and feather you for even setting foot in town," said another council member.

"Or at least for expecting to be the ruler again," a third man sniffed.

"Come now," said Bertam, who was more soft-spoken than the rest. "We could allow him to advise the council on occasion. He has experience he could lend to our discussions."

"He'll want his vote to count for three people," said the first man.

"His voice will count for none," I said, surprised to hear myself speak so suddenly. "I agree that he may have wisdom to share, just as I do. You don't have to listen to us, though."

My husband flashed a meek smile of thanks. In the end, the council ruled that we could both act as non-voting advisers. I assumed he'd burned a few bridges before I arrived, but I was certain this exercise in democracy had shrunken his ego, which was a good thing. I shook his hand as I left the meeting and wished him well.

"Thank you for speaking for me," he said. "I didn't think things would be so different upon my return. My wife warned me about that."

"It will be a pleasure to act as an adviser with you," I said, giving him a nod before I ventured into the darkening streets to find a boardinghouse for the night.

The next day I would secure work as a seamstress and more steady accommodations. It felt good to be back in the old body. Maybe I'd always been an old woman disguised as a young one and never realized it before. The skin was warm and pleasantly wrinkled, like a comfortable shirt. In only a matter of weeks it would be my own. I didn't mind that at all.

Berchta

I WOULDN'T HAVE picked this shade of blue, but, looking at it now, it kind of works. The couch belonged to my grandma, and clashes brilliantly with everything in my living room. I like bright colors and have the sort of fashion taste any interior designer would call a disaster, but there's a reason I have no interior designer friends.

The couch smells like Grandma's condo, a mixture of carpet deodorizer and laundry detergent. It reminds me of sleepovers and popcorn parties and roast chicken suppers, and it's the closest I can get to my grandma now that she's been gone for three months and the contents of her life doled out to kids and grandkids. I inherited the couch and a German hymnal I can't read, but I'm happy with them.

I settle down on the middle cushion with a bag of microwave popcorn to watch TV, but there's a knock on my door. I don't get much company so visitors make me a little excited and a little worried. I find an older lady standing in the hall. She wears a pink sweatsuit, carries a pink tote bag, and has her hair pulled back in a neat bun.

"Can I help you?" I say. I've never seen her before. Maybe she's selling Avon.

The lady peers over my shoulder and grins.

"I found you," she says, skirting past me to the couch and plopping down on the center cushion like she owns it.

"That's my new couch," I say, pivoting around. "Well, it's my grandma's old couch."

"Uh-huh," she says, looking around my living room like she's admitting to this fact but it doesn't make any difference. "You could do with a good dusting and run a vacuum over the carpet. All sorts of crumbs down there."

"That's not the point," I say as I walk over to her. "This is my couch."

"If you must know," she says in a low voice, "I had to find the couch because of the little people. They're from the old country."

My stomach tenses, but I assume she can't be serious until a small person, perhaps eight inches high, crawls out from under the left sofa cushion and sits next to the old woman. He wears dark pants, a long-sleeved cream-colored shirt, and a newsboy cap—a middle-aged elf with a comfortable paunch.

"There you go," she says, patting his shoulder with two fingers. "I've been looking all over for you fellows. Half expected you wouldn't have survived all those decades without regular helpings of meat and potatoes."

"We like pizza now," says the little person. "Pizza and nachos. And we've grown accustomed to lighter beers. All immigrants have to adapt to the new world, I guess, but we've had nearly a century to do it."

"This explains where the chips went last night," I say, easing myself down on the arm of the couch.

My grandma had told me stories about German little people, but I thought they lived underground. Sometimes they were helpful, sometimes they were mischievous, usually they were hungry, but so is the old woman, because they both start munching on my bag of microwave popcorn.

Soon they're joined on the couch by two more pointy-eared little people, who explain they hitched a ride in my great-great-grandmother's steamer trunk when she came over from

Germany. They lived in her couch for years, and my grandma had a hell of a time convincing them to move to a new one when the first was threadbare.

"We've been in the family for years," he says, "you just didn't know it."

"I've been searching for them for decades," says the old lady. "But after this snack we have to do some cleaning."

It takes me another second to realize who she is. Grandma always said Berchta would find me if I didn't keep my room, and later my apartment, tidy. Berchta starts removing cleaning supplies from her tote bag. Like anything else could have been inside.

When I was little my grandma told me all the old stories she'd learned from her grandmother, including ones about Berchta. She was the ugly old woman responsible for making sure people weren't lazy. During the twelve days after Christmas when spirits and trolls roamed the earth, Berchta came down from the mountains to make sure everyone had done their work for the year. She traveled the countryside in a wooden cart, giving gifts to those who'd been industrious and scolding those who hadn't worked hard.

I was more afraid of Berchta looking over my shoulder than I was of Santa, because she seemed nitpicky and I was horrible at keeping my room clean. But she was supposed to be a hideous crone with a hook nose, not a plump woman in a pink jogging suit who looked like somebody's great-aunt.

"You could have soaked the breakfast dishes before you went to work this morning," Berchta says when she drags me to my kitchen. "Dried-on cereal is difficult to get out of bowls."

"I thought you'd bug me about the laundry," I say.

"That's this weekend," she says as she fills the mop bucket.

We clean and clean and clean until my kitchen reeks of pine and lemon, then we have leftover pizza for dinner. The little people eat on the couch while Berchta and I eat at the kitchen table, and she relaxes enough to grouse about how no one appreciates the old gods and goddesses anymore. I assume this is a typical complaint among mythical figures.

"Why do I even bother?" she says. "No one is nervous about the fact I might appear in their living rooms."

"I was," I say.

"Fat lot of good that did," she says.

I decide to shut up because she has a point.

"I should get involved with a charity," she says. "Maybe one that cleans houses after natural disasters. That's always a big mess."

Normally I'm too tired for cleaning when I get home, since I have to keep things spotless at the Italian restaurant where I work. I know more than I'd like to about strict health codes. It seems like I spend half my day covered in flour from mixing and shaping doughs, and the other half wiping down stainless steel equipment and countertops. I love my job—the smell of yeast, the smooth feel of kneaded dough, the wood smoke from the pizza oven. I don't mind the cleaning part, but at home I slack since I live alone and don't care what things look like. At least that used to be the case.

THE NEXT DAY I bring home more extra pizza than usual—we get to eat the mistake pies—but it's just enough for me and Berchta and the little people. I'm not sure how long they plan on staying, but the little people don't have anywhere else to go.

"We came with the couch," they say with a shrug. "We've always lived there."

Berchta doesn't want to leave now that she's found other German speakers and an apartment that needs a good cleaning. I go to my bedroom when I need peace and a nap. Our dishwasher at the restaurant just quit so I had an exhausting day as pizza-maker and pie-pan scraper.

I wake up to the smell of breakfast—hash browns and bacon and coffee—and realize I was so exhausted that I slept through the night. When I mention the open dishwashing position to Berchta, she perks up. It may be one of the least fun jobs in the world, but she says she needs a way to keep busy and be appreciated.

"I got tired of punishing people for not keeping tidy," she says. "Being a feared hag may be fun for a couple of centuries, but then it gets old."

She'd rather be everybody's neatnik grandmother in the corner of the kitchen, singing old German folk tunes while scouring the huge kettles we use for pizza sauce. Everyone thinks she's adorable. My boss is a seventy-one-year-old Italian woman, and she and Berchta get along terribly well. She learned how to cook from her grandma, and gives long kitchen lectures on how no one is connected to their heritage anymore. Berchta agrees. Over coffee and almond cookies on break, they swap recipes and talk about their respective old countries. It makes me miss my grandma more, and think of all the questions I should have asked her but didn't.

EVEN THOUGH MY apartment has never been so clean, I'm a bit upset when Berchta brings home Belsnickle.

"Look who I found at the grocery store," she says, dragging the old troll into my kitchen. I remember him from my grandma's tales. He was St. Nick's Christmas counterpart, but carried a switch to beat bad children. Grandma said he never actually hit kids, he just scared them into submission, but with one glance at Belsnickle I understand how that could have worked. He wears torn jeans, an old T-shirt, a beat-up fedora, and a grumpy expression.

"He needs a good bath and a good meat stew with lots of potatoes," says Berchta.

Belsnickle grunts, gives me a mean glare, and lets himself be towed to the bathroom.

"Don't let him frighten you, honey," Berchta says when she returns. The shower is running so I assume Belsnickle is making himself clean enough to suit her standards. "He's a nice man, he just can't show it. Has an image to protect, you know."

I nod slowly as she chatters about her plans to get him a job as a bouncer at the bar down the street from the Italian restaurant. Once he has a clean suit, a new fedora, and a new switch, he'll look very much like a nasty old uncle you don't want to mess with.

Mealtimes at my apartment take on an interesting dynamic, as Berchta chats with everyone about what she's going to make for dinner tomorrow, Belsnickle grunts at her and me, and the little people on the couch fight over the remote control (in German). I'm not sure how I became an ethnic neighborhood in three weeks' time. Here I am, fifth-generation German, can't read a word of the language, and I'm being lectured by an old goddess on how she'll teach me to make sauerkraut this weekend.

"Cabbage and coarse salt layered in a big bucket," she says. "It's easy and delicious."

I wish Grandma were still here because even though her grandparents were the ones who had come over, she felt alienated from the old country. She couldn't talk very well with her grandparents, who only spoke German, and when her parents wanted to discuss things in secret they spoke the old language like it was a secret code. She told me this sadly when we made lebkuchen, the Christmas cookie I loved because it was my main connection to my heritage.

I have friends who tell the same story—they make tamales or pierogis or homemade pasta with their grandmothers and don't mind that they've been mixed into the Great American Stewpot where the potatoes taste like the carrots taste like the onions taste like the celery. A shame, but now that the old country has invaded my living room, I spend evenings listening to Belsnickle's stories about kids he scared into behaving, and Berchta's stories about people she scared into cleaning their homes. They snicker and sip tea and tell me about old traditions—Easter trees decorated with colored eggs, bonfires on the summer solstice, wearing new clothes on New Year's Day, leaving shoes out on December 6th for Saint Nikolaus to fill with candy.

During our afternoons off, Berchta and I make sauerbraten and honey cookies and potato salad and Christmas breads and spaetzle. I write down the recipes because she never did before, only added a little of this and a little of that until the mixture tasted right. My fridge crammed with German food, I feel like I don't taste so much like everyone's else's stew, but like pumpernickel and honey cookies. These are scraps of heritage my great-great-grandparents would have stuffed into my hands and told me to sew into my American patchwork life.

MY NEW ROOMMATES would be great if I didn't live above the crabbiest man on the face of the planet. He's seventy-something and been in the building forever. While he's never complained about me before, one day I get a call from my landlord saying that my neighbor has reported "excessive foot traffic, stomping, and moving furniture."

I say I had overnight guests and it won't happen again, then I hang up the phone and curse a few times. I know from the people who live on either side of my downstairs neighbor that he's a picky jerk, and seems determined to have the whole apartment building to himself. Allegedly he's made two people move out because they got sick of his bellyaching.

When I see him downstairs at the mailboxes I try to be nice, smile and say hello. He grunts back. He's also a grade school friend of my landlord, and while my landlord is much nicer than my neighbor, they often get coffee at the café on the corner. I'd like to complain about the volume of my downstairs neighbor's complaints—I often hear him ranting on the phone over excessive noise made by other tenants in the hall—but I don't think my landlord would be sympathetic. I love everything else about my apartment. The rent is reasonable, it's the perfect walking distance from work, and my neighbors are nice except for that one, but all it takes is one person to make everything else go to hell.

After the noise complaints, my landlord calls because the downstairs neighbor has been bellyaching over the smell of vinegar and pepper coming through his air vents. He's also sure I have pets. I say that's not the case, and my landlord can come inspect the apartment if he wants. He says that's okay, he believes me, just try to tone down the noise and odors.

"Of course," I say, then hang up the phone and explain the situation to Berchta and Belsnickle and the little people. They say they understand.

"We'll be quieter and I'll keep the windows open when I'm cooking," she says. "We don't want to be a bother to anyone."

I PUT MY foot down when Berchta brings home the dragon. She says she found him wandering around City Park, but I'm not sure if I believe that.

"There's no room for him," I say, though the dragon is nuzzling my hand and looking at me with big black pleading dragon eyes. He's as big as a Newfoundland dog, and my lease agreement says no pets.

"He's very clean and well-mannered," says Berchta. "And he's traumatized, poor fellow. Been living alone for too long with no friends." She goes on to explain how Siegfried killed the dragon's great-great-great-grandfather and bathed in his blood. ("An unnecessarily cruel and messy affair.") His family has been highly traumatized ever since.

Since Belsnickle is bedding down on my recliner chair, Berchta suggests the dragon can sleep in the bathtub. She claims dragon dung (fewmints) is easy to clean up and would make excellent fertilizer for the plants she's started to grow on my fire escape.

"Fewmints smell a little like bay leaves," she says, "and the dragon needs companionship."

I agree reluctantly, then she insists that the dragon come to work with us the next day.

"He hates to be alone," she whispers. "The poor thing worries people will kill him for his blood. All dragons in his line have PTSD, honey. Dragon parents tell their young ones too many bedtime horror stories of knights and wizards. They're convinced the world is out to get them."

Or at least it's out to get a healthy gallon or two of their blood. I say it's okay with me, but she has to explain the situation to our boss. While she's sweet and grandmotherly, I'm not sure how this will sit with her. A wood-fired pizza oven lit by a dragon would be a great thing to advertise, but might violate pesky health codes.

My boss loves the dragon right away—she scratches the dragon behind his ears and says he's adorable—but she's antsy about having an uncontrolled flame indoors. Berchta smiles and says that's easily solved, since we can let him sit behind the restaurant where we have a smoker and outdoor grill. Both are tended by an economics-professor-turned-award-winning-barbe-cue-pit-master named Marcus.

"He reminds me of a Great Dane I used to have," says Marcus, rubbing the side of the dragon's neck. The dragon lets out a low rumble that's something like a cat's purr. "Of course he can sit with me. If the coals go out, I'll just ask him for a little puff."

When I take a break in the middle of the afternoon, I find them sitting on lawn chairs with glasses of iced tea. Marcus tells the dragon about his trips to China to meet with business leaders, and asks the dragon if he's ever met Chinese dragons.

"I've heard they're supposed to be very wise," says Marcus.

The dragon shakes his head but looks intrigued. I feel reassured as I go back inside to tend my own fires in the pizza oven.

The only problem with the new dragon is that he has nightmares. When I get up in the middle of the night to go to the bathroom, I find him whimpering and cowering in the bathtub.

"Are knights invading your dreams again?" I mumble.

The dragon nods his small green head and whines like a scared dog. There's no room for him in the living room, so I sigh and let him come back to my bedroom and sleep at the foot of my bed. The dragon curls into a tight green ball of scales and sighs contentedly. It takes a good bit of effort for the dragon to breathe flame—it's not like every stray sneeze or snort catches things on fire—so I'm not too worried. It's just another thing I'll have to hide from my landlord.

IN THE END Berchta's clean streak proves to be her downfall. When my downstairs neighbor thumps upstairs to complain about the music and dancing and incessant loud vacuuming, I'm at the grocery store. I trust my roommates to behave appropriately, but Berchta vacuums a lot and I have an older model that's pretty loud. I should have sent her door-to-door in her spare time as a volunteer cleaning lady, not left them to the mercy of the guy downstairs.

As it turns out he's also scared of lizards, so the scene is rather chaotic when he pounds on the door and Berchta opens it to reveal the dragon, three little people, and Belsnickle sitting on the couch. He screams loud enough to be heard all the way across the Atlantic.

At least that's what the lady across the hall told me when I got home, arms loaded with grocery bags. My downstairs neighbor thundered away to call the landlord. Berchta frowned and closed the door. When my landlord and cranky neighbor returned, they pounded on my door but no one answered. When they opened it, everyone was gone. So was my couch.

"I swore I didn't see a thing and the fellow downstairs was probably just tired," says the lady across the hall, patting my shoulder and giving me a wink. "But I'm very sorry."

I drag into my oddly empty living room and sit on the armchair since I no longer have a couch. At least Berchta and Belsnickle and the little people and the dragon escaped. Then I realize I need to put away the groceries before the ice cream melts.

When I was living alone before, I was fine with my own company, but this evening I just feel lonely. The apartment is too quiet and empty, even after I rearrange the furniture to make up for the lost couch. I have honey cookies for dinner and call in sick to work the next day. Since I have a massive headache and feel like I'm going to throw up half the time, it isn't exactly a lie.

Seeing the empty bathtub makes me want to cry, even though it's never been so clean.

A day later when I return to work and the pizza oven, I have to explain to my boss and Marcus that Berchta and the dragon left. I say they went back to the old country, since I hope that's what happened. If not, at least they were all together, so they can roam the wild streets and pizza joints of the new world with friends. It's hard not to cry when I see a new person at the dishwashing station, but I have to wipe my eyes on my wrist and make more pizza dough.

That night when I get home I realize I'm out of cookies so I drag myself to the kitchen and plan on digging through the fridge for sad leftovers. Then I see what Berchta left on one of my chairs at the table—her pink tote of cleaning supplies and a whole stack of recipes that I copied down as she cooked. I flip through the cards until I find one for lebkuchen. I get out the flour and honey and sugar and eggs and candied fruit and a large mixing bowl, humming one of those old German songs and wondering if she'll ever return for a visit. I'll need to have sauerkraut ready, and the kitchen should be spotless. Or maybe I'll just try to mop more often.

Body Spirits

WHEN I SEE the short pointy-eared guy clinging to my dad's shoulders I mistake him for a demon, but realize that can't be right because demons have horns, at least I think that's how it works. Then the imp sticks its ice pick between my dad's vertebrae, so I figure it's a back gremlin. This clears up a couple of questions, like why my dad has been cranky. It's not me, it's that he's got an ice pick sticking out of his back, so while he can only grunt as we have dinner, his mood has become much more excusable. I stop by the drugstore the next day since I need some extra-strength pain relievers, and buy a bottle for him and a heating pad. Dad grunts a thank-you when I drop off the pad and pills, but I don't stay long since I have to go home and deal with my arthritis witch.

She sticks pins in my fingers and elbows and knees—well, mostly my fingers—meaning I have to stop typing or filing patient records and rub on Aspercreme. You can't get much done with pins in your fingers, though I do a lot despite them, but I take an early coffee break and talk with my witch.

"You don't have to go full steam all the time," she says, leaning over my shoulder to insert another needle in my index finger joint. When I'm at the office I can only sigh, but at home

I stop cooking or reading and make a mug of tea to hold and soothe my hands.

"You'd never stop working if it weren't for me," she says as we sit on the couch with our tea. I make a mug for her, too, since I'd rather not be on her bad side. She's sticking pins in me as it is.

"Guess not," I grumble, clutching the mug and its brief comfort. I've gained sympathy for other people who I see walking around with arthritis witches, though they tend to be older than me. I glimpse them in the grocery store, riding those little scooters and reaching for cans of soup. If there's a gaggle of witches clustered around them with pins and darning needles, I ask if I can help. Sometimes they say yes and sometimes no, but either way I feel like I shouldn't ignore them.

Some days the pain is so bad, grit-my-teeth-so-I-don't-scream bad, that I think my witch is using pickaxes instead of needles. But I've learned that body spirits never kill you, they just feel like they could, and maybe someday they will, but not yet. My witch and I have truces that last for days or weeks or months at a time, when she sits just behind my right shoulder and only offers the occasional jab. I live with the all-too-human comfort of knowing that everyone winds up with witches or demons or imps, but I'm only thirty-five and other people, at least ones my age, can't see the arthritis witch, which doesn't help on days when I move like I'm seventy. Maybe I even feel like I'm seventy, though I worry that by the time I reach that age, my witch will have multiplied.

But she doesn't scare me like the blond guy who hangs out with my boyfriend. The blond elf is a pale young man who wears jeans and backward ball caps. Usually he keeps his hands in his pockets, but sometimes he taps my boyfriend on the shoulder and whispers things in his ear—brilliant things, my boyfriend says. They smile at each other, then my boyfriend drops to his knees and convulses on the ground, or shakes in his desk chair for agonizing seconds. Even when he pees his pants or bites his tongue so it bleeds, he says the inspirations and insights the blond guy gives him are so wonderfully fantastic, it's worth a faint and a little blood.

I've asked him to please, please, please take his medications because then he wouldn't fall down so often and risk hitting his head on the floor, or pavement, but he just kisses my forehead.

"I know there's a risk," he says, "but if you could understand those moments of clarity..." He trails off and stares into a space above my head that must be so beautiful, so colorful, it's totally infuriating.

Often his trembling isn't bad—he shivers for fifteen or twenty or thirty seconds in his desk chair, his eyes closed, and then he comes to. When he falls I turn him to his side so he doesn't choke if he throws up, and stick the handle of a plastic spoon between his teeth so he doesn't bite his tongue. Then I lie or sit beside him until he shakes his head like waking from a dream. He's taken to wearing disposable underwear in case he has a bladder malfunction at work. He says astronauts wear them, too.

"Don't call them adult diapers," he says, so I don't.

But I know he could get hurt during a longer time of trembling, and this is why he takes showers instead of baths so he doesn't drown, and why I worry about him driving. During the day I use the car, and he walks to work at a digital archive downtown. They scan records for families and historical societies and organizations so thousands of documents can be stored on a tiny thumb drive instead of all those boxes. Sometimes he makes digital copies of almost-falling-apart books, and wears white gloves. He says the lighting is perfect and doesn't bother him. In bad weather—too rainy or icy or cold—I drive him to the archive and kiss him goodbye and tell him to call me if anything happens.

"I will," he says, but he never does. His boss has called twice, and I've heard my boyfriend in the background saying there's no need to worry, he's fine. I think about him for the rest of the day.

At the dental clinic I don't want to see the assorted spirits and various devices they have clamped around our patients' heads and mouths, things that look like vises with teeth. I smile at our patients, say *How are you*, give them the clipboard with a pen and the proper forms, then look back down at my desk calendar before I get nauseated. I am the first to volunteer for typing in new patient data or adding to records when we get behind, though too much keyboarding makes my fingers hurt. What doesn't?

MY BOYFRIEND IS a photographer, takes pictures of clouds and trees and squirrels in the grove of trees near our apartment building, then he plays with the images in a photo-editing program to blur the bird feeders and overly large pine trees. His landscapes seem like a hazy fairy world. I don't know whether the grove seems more magical or eerie when he finds spaceships whizzing through the branches, but he says those moments of darkness and trembling are how he gets his best ideas. My boyfriend claims the medications he's been prescribed to make the blond guy go away make him feel tired and dizzy, blurring his vision, so the last thing he wants to do when he gets home from work is experiment with photography projects.

"Would you want to take a pill that made you feel like throwing up?" he asks.

"We could try something else," I say.

"Everything is worse than the shaking," he says. "At least it's interesting."

But I don't trust the tall blond guy. My boyfriend has had work in local art shows and galleries and thinks of the blond guy as a muse, though he doesn't say so. I have no one to discuss this with but my arthritis witch, who isn't much help. She says sometimes brilliance hurts.

"Your boyfriend isn't the first person to honor his trembling," she says. "Other composers and writers and artists have said the same." And maybe they were all talking with an angel, or a chimera, or some other spirit in the burst of euphoria before collapse.

"You have to think of the ways we can be helpful. Like how I make you slow down and think before you do things." My witch links her elbow with mine.

"You're a major pain," I say.

"A pain that makes you reflective," she says. "A pain that makes you careful."

"Because everything hurts," I say.

"And don't I always let you know about air pressure changes?" she continues.

"Like a fucking barometer," I say.

"Damn straight," she says, then she adds, "Seriously, you're not going to make him change his mind about this. They're too close."

The difference is I would get rid of her if I could, but he won't get rid of that imp or sprite or whatever it is.

"I wouldn't need so many pins if you didn't stress yourself out over him," my witch says, jabbing another in my finger joint. Sometimes my hands look like porcupines, and she blames me for it. Or we blame me together. I should eat less sugar and butter and cheese. More broccoli and garlic and turmeric to reduce inflammation. Exercise, exercise, exercise.

I SEE OTHER people with spirit companions they don't seem to mind, like folks who have imps sitting on their foreheads holding glasses in front of their face, lenses that make the world brighter or darker or blurred. When older people with imps on their heads walk into the dental clinic, I ask if they'd like help filling out paperwork—usually they nod because the print is so teeny-tiny—but once I chatted with a lady at my coffee shop who had a white cane and grew up with her imps who held wonderful pink cat's eye frames in front of her face. She said she saw shapes and colors and movement, but had learned how to cook by touch and smell. She'd also learned braille when she was a kid, and said it was great since she could read in the dark while her boyfriend was sleeping.

Then there are the two guys I see at the library when I go there on Sundays. They have earmuff pixies sitting on their heads. One guy's earmuffs are small and blue and look satiny, like tiny pillows, while the other guy's earmuffs are large and purple and invitingly fuzzy. The pixies hold the earmuffs in place while the guys' hands weave walls of words between them. I've stared at them a few times, trying not to but it looks so beautiful, that dance of fingers. I wish I could understand what they're saying, but before I get the courage to tap one of them on the shoulder and wave, my arthritis witch pokes my fingers again, so I rub them and wonder if they could stand that kind of aerobic workout.

WHEN WE GO to my parents' house for dinner, my dad grouses about his latest trip to the doctor, a guy who's suggested back surgery, something about a herniated disk, which makes Dad and his back gremlin grimace, though for different reasons. Dad does not want scalpels in his spine since he already has the ice pick. I say he should get another opinion because usually you can improve back problems with exercises and physical therapy a couple times a week. Dad frowns and nods. The gremlin frowns. He does not want to be shaken. I'm sure that next, snakes will start eating my parents' hearts, plugging up arteries with their too-long tails, and Mom will notice the pain but think it's just heartburn.

I don't see my boyfriend's elf at dinner, but he's there in the evening when we sit on the couch to watch TV. He waits on my boyfriend's other side, winking at me as he leans to whisper something in his ear. If I could grab him by that T-shirt collar, drag him out of the living room. and throw him out the door I would, but I know if I tried, the fabric would glide through my aching fingers and he'd laugh.

The elf keeps his hand on my boyfriend's knee, wants to take him from me, is reaching some nook just behind his heart that I can't touch. I suppose this is how it's always happened—elves spirit your loved one to their realm and keep them there forever, the only difference being this particular realm is inside my boyfriend's head.

My witch is too calm about his possession, sticking me with pins when we take our daily walk downtown on my lunch break. Walking is supposed to help my arthritis, though sometimes that just means longer discussions with the witch. Other times I give up on constructive conversation, just eat my steamed broccoli and drink turmeric tea. She ignores that these foods are supposed to ward her off. I know my witch is genetic—my grandma and grandpa both had arthritis witches, though I was just a little kid and couldn't see them. My doctor says that sometimes people inherit weak cartilage, and witches. No drug has proven effective against them, though they're working on clinical witch-prevention trials.

"I have patients who played sports in high school, usually football, and their knees are killing them by the time they're thirty," she explains, then offers a cortisone shot I know will keep my witch at bay for a few days. It's not a long break, but I take it and drive home with my witch in the passenger seat, her arms crossed.

When I get back to the apartment my boyfriend isn't there, and for a moment I worry he passed out at work and had to go to the hospital and nobody called to tell me, but then I see the note on the kitchen table. He's out taking pictures. I ease myself into a chair, bright with the fear that someday the elf will take my boyfriend and not bring him back. I know this is rare, but I've researched a little about the spirits of medicine, the side effects of elves, how trembling can steal his memories over time. What if he forgets that he loves me? I know this sounds teenage and dramatic, but it makes perfect sense late at night when we're lying in bed and I want to ask, *Do you love me? How about now? How about now?* How to describe the anger and embarrassment and fear when he slithered to the floor last month in the grocery store and started to tremor and I had to grab the plastic comb from my purse to stick in his mouth so he didn't bite his tongue?

My boyfriend returns from his photography session and kisses me hard on the mouth, says he got some great pictures, but later that night when we're cuddling on the couch and watching a movie, the elf interrupts with one of his thought explosions. I feel my boyfriend tremble against me, his eyes rolled back so he can see that other world inside his head, the one that appears in his photographs. I grab a spoon from my cup of tea and jam it between his teeth. He drools slightly. No stain appears in his crotch, so I assume he's wearing disposable underwear. He blinks, coming back to me, but I have never been so angry at the elf for interrupting what was supposed to be a calm Friday cuddle. He has no boundaries. I have to stop him.

The pills my boyfriend's doctor prescribed are in the medicine cabinet, untouched except for four. I crush one and mix it with raspberry jam the way my mom did with baby aspirin when I was a kid, then spread the jam on cornbread muffins. Raspberry seeds and crushed pills have an identical crunch, and he loves cornbread. At breakfast he barely looks at what he's eating while flipping through an art magazine, aware enough to know there's food in front of him.

And maybe over the next few days he's not as...sharp? He goes to work. He comes home from work. He lazes on the couch, still as sleep. His boss doesn't call me to report tremoring. I remind myself this is not betrayal, this is a way to save him, because each time you hit your head and bash your brain it matters, at least according to my doctor. I've told my boyfriend that, but he doesn't care.

I don't see the elf, though my boyfriend spends the weekend curled on the couch staring at the TV. A few times he goes to the bathroom. I hear water running, the toilet flush, he mumbles about having the flu and I shouldn't get too close. I ask if he's hungry, give him more muffins with jam. I know I shouldn't be doing this, but I balance the fact that I'm a horrible person with potentially saving his cranium and his life. His body will take a while to get used to the pills, the absence of that elf. His flu drags into a fourth day. A fifth. A sixth. He misses work.

But this is a cure, not poison. I return home to find him curled on the couch. If we went to his doctor she would probably suggest another medication, one that might work better, but he'll refuse to go. And I might have to admit what's in the jam.

I can let him be sick, or I can let him tremble.

I wish I could go with him to that space, wish I could understand how it could be so enchanting, if there are fireworks and a flower garden and the brightest stars you could imagine, a universe of light. Maybe I'm jealous because the elf takes him and not me, never me, I'm stuck here with my arthritis witch and her endless pincushion.

After a week and a half of living with my fuzzy-headed boyfriend who doesn't want to sit in front of the computer or even pick up his camera, I give him back to the elf. I've made him hang his poor head over a toilet for several hours, so of course he'll be happy to return to those bursts of euphoria. I should feel guilty for trying the pills on him. I don't.

"What else is there to do but relent?" my witch says as I pound down the sidewalk on my lunchtime walk. I ignore her. She makes a jab with the pins, but sometimes misses. I will fight her off with spears of broccoli and floods of turmeric tea. I will hug my boyfriend tight after his tremors, threading my achy fingers through his. I will hold my boyfriend until he opens his eyes, blinks and smiles, then I'll make tea for both of us, and pile a plate with cookies, a reminder of how often being in a body is equal parts pleasure and negotiation.

The Pieces

WHEN MY MOTHER calls after breakfast on Saturday morning, she's using the extremely calm tone of voice she only employs when something has gone terribly wrong. After the basic "Hello" and "How are you?" she says, "Well, it's finally happened. Your father has gone to pieces, or had a nervous breakdown. I'm not sure which, but you should probably come over."

I was at my parents' house a week ago for dinner since it was my dad's birthday. We had chocolate cake and Dad looked morose, but he always gets depressed on his birthday. Mom says he's doing a life inventory, pondering what he's done so far and what he can do in his remaining years and if it will be enough to justify his time on the earth and the resources he's consumed.

I had thought my father was just sitting with a crossword at the kitchen table, but now I realize he's been considering mortality, the additions and subtractions that make life worth living. He seems too young for that, then I realize he's only six years younger than my grandfather was when he died, and he's already outlived his own grandfather who had heart problems at sixty-two. What equations does my dad do in his head and not tell us about?

"He's in the living room," Mom says when I arrive.

When I walk through the door I see my father has indeed gone to pieces like a decapitated doll torn apart by an angry kid. I did that to my Barbies, but I was playing Civil War field doctor and performing amputations. Because she is tidy and meticulous, my mother has lined up the parts of my father against the wall—both his legs, his arms, the lower torso, the upper torso and shoulders, and his head.

"Um, hi," I say.

"Hello," says my father's head with a sigh. His fingers give me a wiggle of greeting.

"How are you feeling?" I say.

"Been better, been worse."

I don't ask when he has been worse, which isn't to say I'm not curious about it.

"Should we call a doctor or something?" I ask.

"I don't know how they could help." My father often gets mad at doctors. "They'll tell me this is just one of those things that happens when you get older and I have to wait it out."

"Can I get you anything?" I say.

"Go have lunch with your mother, she's hungry," he says in a slightly accusatory tone, like being hungry is my mother's fault. "Leave me here for a moment. I need to think."

I return to the kitchen, surprised since this is a tidier explosion than I expected. There are weeks when it seems like my dad is always on the verge of combusting, like someone planted land mines in his brain and we have to be careful to walk around them. He doesn't tell us what he's dwelling on, just gets upset and lashes out because nobody can do anything right.

Last week when my mother wrote "oregano" on the shopping list, Dad said, "We already have a new jar of oregano in the spice cupboard," in a tone like this was a personal affront. We do not try to understand him, just study him like careful biologists or heavy weapons technicians.

"It's just been that time of the month for him," my mom says with a shrug. "Let's make quiche. I've been wanting to try your recipe forever." Dad has been possessive of cooking since he retired from teaching. Mom wants to cook, too, but stays out of the kitchen to be on the safe side. Sometimes I worry she has to think about the safe side too much.

From the living room Dad calls, "When's the date for your wedding?"

"We don't have one," I say, which he already knows.

"Why not?" he says. "What if you or your boyfriend are in an accident and the other one needs visitation rights for the hospital?"

Don't get me wrong, my dad is a loving person. When I was a little kid he'd lie on the carpet and hold me in his hands above his body. I'd flap my arms and giggle, trying to fly like a bird.

But sometimes he'd get upset for something small, like how I took three cookies for dessert when I was only supposed to have two.

"Aren't you listening to your mother?" he yelled as I cowered behind a counter and didn't want cookies anymore.

Other times when we went on road trip vacations, he'd get upset about Chicago traffic and be snippy the rest of the day, making Mom and me wonder why we tried to have fun around him. I can list all his primary rants over the past fifteen years:

Why did I attend just one semester of college?

Why didn't I go back to school after I lost my job at the hardware store?

Why didn't I go back to school after the shoe store closed?

What do I plan on doing with my life now that I've been unemployed for four months? Do I want to live in a cardboard box?

The last one hurt. I left without speaking to him and went home to my boyfriend, who said that when people get mad they say things they don't mean. I know that, but my dad doesn't realize how his words are a slap that stings forever. Mom and I don't forget, though we're sure he does.

I make the quiche filling and Mom makes the crust and we slide the pie plate in the oven and wait. We don't want to go back to the living room with the pieces of my father. Sometimes it's easier to leave him alone, so she makes tea and we sit at the kitchen table.

"At least it wasn't a heart attack," says my mother.

"I wonder how long it takes to recover from something like this," I say.

"We'll have to take his lower torso to the bathroom sometimes," she says, "when he lets me know. It's nice to cook again. Since he got out of that basement workshop, I can't get him out of the kitchen."

My dad was a high school math teacher who always wanted to be an inventor, but it never worked out. He spent a long time in his basement lab, soldering things and swearing and waiting for someone to recognize his genius, but it never quite happened. You have to be in the right place at the right time with the right people needing the thing you came up with. Dad never wanted to go on the road with his gizmos, wasn't big on self-promotion, which makes being an inventor more difficult. His ideas came in obsessive phases. For a while it was jar lids and how to make them hard for kids and easy for people with arthritis to open. Then he was working on devices to help visually impaired people read, but inventors with more money and better computer skills were always a little ahead of him.

The oven buzzes, the quiche is finished, and I'm starved.

"Did you put peas in it?" says my dad.

"Of course we did," I say. "Mom and I both like peas."

"Why did you have to ruin a good quiche like that?" he says.

"I take it this means you don't want any," I say.

"Not if there's going to be peas in it," says Dad.

"More for us then," I say.

This is my father in a bad mood. When that happens he casts a pall over the world and no one can do anything right. My mother is a part-time saint for living with him, but as a children's librarian she's honed her skills to withstand toddler hurricanes and my father. I think she's spent the better part of her life trying to decode him. It's part psychology, part genetics, part biochemistry, and part theorizing with me over coffee.

We both have two pieces of quiche, save the rest for dinner, and congratulate ourselves on a lunch well done.

"Can you stay with him this afternoon?" she asks. "I need to go to the store and run a few other errands."

I take a deep breath and nod, then sit with Dad in the living room and try to make conversation.

"My friend Trish is training me how to do makeup for dead people," I say, "so maybe I can work part-time at her parents' funeral home." I smile since I've never liked putting makeup on my face, but other people are different. Easier. They're also dead so they can't complain if I use a little too much blush.

"When will that be a real job?" Dad says. "Right now your boyfriend is stopping you both from living in a cardboard box."

I purse my lips and remind myself that Dad is grumpy and scared and we should get out of the house since we need a distraction. I decide to take Dad out for coffee, and start loading his upper and lower torso into the back seat of my car.

"Why can't we take my arms?" he says. "With them and my head, I can drink coffee on my own."

"I'll get you a straw," I say. "You have good coordination, but not when your arms and head are separate."

Dad does not appreciate the criticism. "They're my arms and I can decide if I need them or not."

"I'm not lugging them out to the car," I say. "If they want to crawl on their own they can be my guest."

His arms look happy against the wall and wave goodbye to us. I carry Dad's head like it was a heavy crystal vase filled with important gray matter. I'm not sure how to secure it in the passenger seat, so I put him in back between the two halves of his torso.

Before we drive to the coffee shop, I call my boyfriend and ask if he wants to have coffee with us. I don't tell him about Dad's current state of embodiment, but I know I'll need help moving all the pieces.

Dad and I don't talk much on the way to the coffee shop, and I'm glad my boyfriend can meet us at the door. He carries the two halves of the torso and I carry the head, so we stack Dad on a chair. My boyfriend sits at the table with him and chats pleasantly, as he can do with anyone under any circumstance. I order our drinks. Iced coffees with straws.

"So have you applied for any other jobs lately?" my dad asks my boyfriend. My boyfriend has his PhD in philosophy and Dad thinks he should be working in the ethics department of a big company, not in a produce section.

"It's a consideration," says my boyfriend mildly. I wonder how he can be so good at deflecting my dad when he didn't grow up with him. Or maybe that's the answer. Dad turns his attention to me, and his usual assertion that I need to go back to school.

"And study what?" I say because we've had this argument a hundred times.

"What do you want to study?"

"I don't have passion for anything," I say. "There's no reason for me to waste money on something I don't like. I don't want to be an accountant or teacher or chef or hairstylist."

"You want to put makeup on dead people," he says.

"And what the hell is wrong with that?" I say.

"You could make more money doing something else."

"Like what?" I say.

"I don't know, that's for you to decide."

"And I'm deciding not to go to college."

We pout at each other. I can see myself reflected in Dad, or Dad reflected in me, the same cheekbones and nose and ears and slightly squinted eyes. We are the same kind of determined. I know he wants me to do well in life. I know he is scared as any parent would be scared about his child's future. But Dad has never been good at expressing that concern in a way that makes me want to do anything but push back. And now he's a head and two blocks of torso stacked on top of each other. For once I am in control.

I could leave him at the coffee shop, but that would not be nice. Because he is my dad. Because I have so many imperfections that it would take hours to list them. Because I love my dad even when he drives me crazy, which happens a lot, but that's why they call it love.

My boyfriend and I take my dad piece by piece back to the car. I kiss my boyfriend, then drive Dad home.

"He's a nice guy," says Dad.

"Great," I say, "since we'll spend the rest of our lives together in a cardboard box."

Dad is quiet for a moment, then he says, "I just want what's best for you."

"And of course I want to screw my life up royally," I say. "According to you, that's been the plan all along."

"I'm sorry if I upset you," he says.

I could say, *You're really good at it, you've had a lot of practice. Don't you realize you've been upsetting me for the better part of thirty-five years?* But I don't say that, because sometimes I can use a slightly wiser part of mind that tells me to respond with "Thank you."

By the time we get home, the two pieces of Dad's torso that my boyfriend stacked together have melded again. I need Mom's help to get him out of the car, but we lay the pieces of Dad on the floor in the living room, putting his arms and legs in place like a jigsaw puzzle and hoping that something good will happen. Mom and I go to the kitchen and make sugar cookies, and I tell her about putting makeup on corpses, which she says sounds very interesting.

Just before dinner my dad walks into the kitchen, shaking his limbs like he's testing them to make sure they're secure.

"May I have a cookie?" he asks. We say sure. He eats two along with a ham sandwich, then says he needs to rest on the couch. Mom and I hear his contented snore, and decide to let sleeping dads lie. We reheat the quiche for dinner, and wonder if a lesson has been learned by anyone. Mom says we can figure that out tomorrow, we've done enough for one day. I tend to agree.

Switching Heads

EIGHT HEADS MIGHT seem like too many, but sometimes I wish I had more. During the day I'll switch four or five times for different tasks, though I still don't have a head that enjoys cleaning, just one that decides the kitchen floor needs to get swept at eleven o'clock at night due to an accumulation of spilled coffee grounds. I suppose compulsion is better than nothing.

Half of the heads want to get married, but the others don't. I tried matrimony once and it didn't work, so the anti-marriage heads figure we shouldn't mess with another ceremony. The rest think Lee is perfect and worth a shot. Lee and I are both thirty-six and have been together for eight years. The anti-marriage heads say why ruin a good thing, but those are the heads I try to wear around Lee so they won't pester about a ring. This is a problem, since I think he likes Four best—she's sassy and speaks her mind, but wants to get hitched.

"Why don't you wear that one more often?" Lee asks me at breakfast. "She'd be a great teacher."

"She'd cuss out the students," I say. I'm wearing Three, which tends to be diplomatic about Four's strengths and weaknesses.

"That wouldn't be a bad thing for some of them."

"Staff meeting this afternoon," I say. "She shouldn't go."

"Well, I like her."

"Except when she asks you about a ring," I say. Lee is in the why-do-we-need-a-damn-certificate-and-ceremony camp, and I am too. Half the time.

"I like everything else about her," Lee says, which includes sex. She's inventive. But as much as she thinks she'd like to get married, she's not the marrying type. Four doesn't compromise, or understand tact, skills that other heads tried to master when we were younger and still hitched. I probably wore Four too much then, which didn't help.

Five and Seven think we need to get rid of Four, or at least use her more judiciously, because she's short on social graces. Without Four I wouldn't be all of me, but I don't know what to do with the parts of myself that are annoying and pushy and most likely to get me fired. That would be fine with Four. She wants to start her own school, or go back to school, or move overseas and teach English in China or Thailand and have adventures. She doesn't care that this contradicts her plans to get married.

My eight heads look the same, aside from the expressions that remain when I take them off and nestle them on the shelf in my closet. When resting they have a slightly different flare to their nostrils, curl to their lips, tension in their cheeks. They've changed temperaments over time, though some, like Four, are more stubborn than others. Some want yogurt and a banana for lunch, others demand a cheeseburger. I carry an extra head in a bowling ball bag, in case I need to change for a staff meeting or after-school appointment. I wish heads could be worn all day, but they weren't designed for it, though I find myself using One, Three, and Seven most during the school year. Three is compassionate, Seven has a no-nonsense demeanor, and One is philosophical, though that means she's best worn after school.

I need a range of heads when it comes to students like Justin, this kid who bangs his elbow on the radiator during fifth period. Usually it's not that loud, but two weeks ago I was talking about weather fronts and snapped at him to quit with the percussion. I was wearing Seven, which tends to be more forthright, and I know he was bothering other students, but all the kids turned to look at him. Justin quit, but was back at it the next day.

He isn't a bad kid—he did well on the weather unit, and loved the tornado in a bottle we made in class—but he often has an unfocused, daydreamy gaze. A lot of kids do in middle school, but not all the time. Some kids have school heads, I'm pretty sure about that, but maybe Justin doesn't, which is why I suggest that he get an aide to take him out of class when he needs a break. I'm not the only teacher who's noticed his tongue clicking and radiator banging and pen chewing. When I explain my proposal in an after-school meeting with his parents and three other teachers, the teachers nod in agreement but his parents twist their mouths into frowns.

They say they don't want him to have an aide, because he would be singled out.

"He's singled out when he's banging his elbow against the radiator," I say.

"He can learn not to do that," says his mother. "You can punish him. He's got to learn how to be in the real world."

If he can't switch heads he can switch environments and be out of my class for a moment—it wouldn't be the first time some kid needed to do that—but to some parents, "aide" is a four-letter word. But I am wearing Three, which nods at the mother's belligerence. Three understands compromise, and working the system, and agreements made quietly with students after class. Three may have a talk with Justin tomorrow. Four would have told the parents to get their heads out of their asses.

After that conference I need a long thinking session, which means taking a walk to the burned-out apartment building a mile from my house. One, my most meditative head, likes to do this when she's pondering a problem. I should loan Justin my weather-related textbooks. He could go in the hall and read. But would he remember to come back to class?

I drag my feet a little when I'm a block away from the apartment complex. I'm never sure if I should come back, but One insists on it. The fire happened six months ago. Fourteen people died, which was deemed tragic enough to make the national news. The building's wiring wasn't up to code, and a lot of the smoke detectors weren't working. I heard the sirens at ten at night, and smelled slight smoke since I had a window open. I figured something bad must have happened, but didn't consider the scale. The middle school lost three students, and one was in my class. Derrick. He loved studying rocks, a rare trait in seventh graders, and he was kind of a jerk. It wasn't the first time I'd lost a student, but this was different because of all the people affected—families, neighbors, the kids at school. Nobody could explain why more people didn't get out.

I stand on the front step and think about Derrick and how much delight he took in saying "schist." He also got detention for chucking rocks at other kids after school. What was I supposed to do with that combination of brilliance and violence?

"Why you out here?" The voice is old, scratchy, but clears its throat. "It's not a damned shrine."

I want to say, *Yes, it is a damned shrine, as long as they haven't demolished it,* but I turn to my inquisitor, a gray-haired lady wearing jeans and a green cardigan, staring at me with her arms crossed.

"Three of the kids who died were my students," I say. "I was thinking about them." I don't know why I decide to claim them all, but maybe claiming one seems like it wouldn't be enough?

"Oh," she says, relaxing her shoulders a bit. "I live across the way, and we get too damn many gawkers out here taking pictures of themselves and the building on their cell phones. The biggest disaster to hit the state in years, and they want to ask me was I here and what did it sound like and wasn't it awful. Well shit, of course it was awful, but I don't want to remember it over and over. Let the dead have a little peace."

I nod. It's strange how scared we are of our own deaths, but we're fascinated by the deaths of others. Another instance of head-switching. But I wouldn't want to live across the street. A mile away lets me keep the memory at a distance.

"They were good kids?" the old lady says.

"Not really," I say. "Well, two of the kids were good kids. The other was a cut-up. He poked at other kids during class, made smart remarks, and got into fights after school. But I kind of liked him."

"Oh," she says, and nods with a certain…appreciation? Curiosity? "My son was a little asshole when he was in junior high, but he turned out okay."

"Middle school is the age to do it," I say. "Sometimes they just kind of lose their heads."

I DON'T KNOW why our new principal, who even Three thinks is an asshole, decides to introduce the new discipline policy in a morning as opposed to an afternoon staff meeting, but he says it's going into effect immediately. We will no longer do in-school suspensions for physical fights between students. Instead, we'll send the kids to the juvenile detention center.

"This policy will send a message that we're serious about cracking down on violence," he says, but I think he's tired of having bullies clog up the detention rooms in the main office. JDC will only give them a wider cohort. If I were wearing Four or Seven I'd say that, because it's what the rest of the teachers are thinking, but wearing Three means I don't need to bite my tongue.

The teachers' lounge consensus is that no one likes the principal. He's the kind of know-it-all boss who has to be right, though he's spent his career in administration. Those ones don't understand students like principals who've had time in the class-room, and while the school board asked for our opinion during the interview process, they only go along with what we say if they agree with it.

At lunch the lounge is buzzing with comments no one made in the faculty meeting when we were wearing our profes-sional heads:

"That place breeds delinquents."

"He can't handle the tough cases, just wants to pawn them off."

"Did he pull shit like this at his last school?"

Professional heads must be removed for at least a half hour in the late morning or early afternoon, or else we would explode from the excess of decorum.

"Some kids figure out they're douchebags sooner, and some of them later," says Jack, who teaches American history and is maybe thirty. He always stays after school to help some kid with their reading assignments. "You hope it's sooner, but we can't do much about it either way."

"All those bullies end up as CEOs or incarcerated," says Harold, who's taught math for forty years and is our resident oracle. For eighty-six percent of bullies he speaks the truth, but I want to do my best with the other fourteen.

Sometimes I think about using Four during after-school meetings with students, so I could look them in the eye and say, "What were you thinking?" I don't want to sound angry, just find out what's going on in their heads.

That's the case with Amber, who sits in the back row during sixth period and reads her science or math book unless we're doing group work, then she sighs and narrows her eyes, pouting to some corner of the room where she sits with her group, arms crossed. When asked to help, she'll shove kids, break pencils, twist arms, pinch hard. She does well enough on tests, a B student, and an average-sized kid who seems like she'll calmly steamroll her way through life. So now Amber will get into a fight, go to JDC, and...read? I've met her mom twice, a tired woman who works at a nursing home and told me to do what I needed to do.

"She had an aide in elementary school, but her dad and I decided no more of that when she got to middle school," Amber's mom said with a shrug. "She has to learn how the world works."

I sympathize with the bullies, which isn't to say I like all of them, I just understand how it feels to forget a head at home, or not bring it on purpose because you don't want to switch. But head-switching is part of growing up, which means talking to people instead of giving them a hard pinch when they ask you, no matter how cattily, to help with the lab assignment. Yet is it ever helpful to punish the pinchers and punchers and social disruptors by sending them to jail-like isolation, or is it most important to protect other kids from harm?

When I get home I'm still frustrated about the JDC proclamation, on top of my usual after-school tired and hungry. I keep Seven on after she decides to make macaroni and cheese for therapeutic reasons—we need comfort food—but while I'm stirring the roux, Lee comes home from work, drops his briefcase on a chair, then puts his hands on my hips and kisses the back of my neck.

"Do we have to eat right away?" he says.

"Macaroni and cheese takes a while to make," I say.

"We could go out."

"I'm boiling water." Seven is not in the mood for amour. She wants to fry a lot of bacon to add to the macaroni and cheese. Lee keeps kissing the back of my neck. When he's stressed and wants sex to calm down, he's persistent as hell. I wish he could change heads—why does it have to be me all the time?—but Seven will capitulate, albeit angrily. I turn off the burners, grab his hand, drag him to the living room, and close the blinds.

"We could go to the bedroom," he says.

"I thought you wanted to do this now," I say, unzipping the back of my skirt.

Our strip is unceremonious. He tries to maintain a smile. I dig my short fingernails into his back, and refuse to orgasm. That would take a while, and I'm hungry. When we get dressed again I leave my pantyhose off, which generally improves my mood.

I relight the burners, stirring the roux as I start to add milk. Lee tiptoes into the kitchen and asks what's wrong, which would have been a better question before sex, but neither of his heads could be bothered to think about that.

"Just a shitty day," I say. "Do I have to explain it?"

"No," he says quietly, touching my hip again as I turn bacon in the frying pan. The fatty odor is comforting, and I'll add onion to soak up the grease. I switch to Three before we eat so I can be more pleasant, but Three starts to ache from the accumulated stress of the day. It isn't as good at venting as a few of my other heads, and is more prone to mulling, lamenting, and feeling guilty. Three is also more conducive to peaceful dinners.

"Feeling any better?" Lee asks.

"A little," I lie to spare his feelings and avoid further questions, but after dinner I might switch to One again and go on another walk. I need a little introspection.

I MEAN TO take Three to school for a parent meeting, but I grab Four instead and only notice when I'm on lunch break. This isn't awful for parent meetings, since most interpret Four's swearing as honesty. But the parent meeting runs late, so I wear Four to the staff meeting since I don't have time to switch. No, that's a lie. I want to wear Four to the staff meeting, or rather, I don't want to take it off.

The principal looks more sour-faced than usual, skips the how-are-you pleasantries, and announces that Jack was arrested for assault last night. He was at a bar, had a physical altercation with another patron, and someone called the police. Jack was released on bail. I close my eyes. He seems too smart for stuff like that, though I mostly know him from teachers' lounge chats. He's divorced, has his four-year-old son on the weekends, and laments about his ongoing battle with student loans.

Assault is bad, but I want to know more of the details. Everyone has their own story when something like this happens. Maybe Jack had enough to drink to act like an asshole, but the other guy might have been the same. Everyone is allegedly innocent until proven guilty, though from the principal's tone Jack might as well have committed grand larceny. I heard through the lounge grapevine that Jack had a few loud words with him last week over the new JDC policy. It wasn't the first time they've had loud words about school policies, but Jack strikes me as an underdog advocate, and the principal believes in the letter of the law. If anyone would have a workplace war, it'd be them.

"I'm going to suggest to the state board of education that this be grounds for an investigation, and possible dismissal or license revocation, based on his previous conduct," says the principal. This statement prompts raised eyebrows and exchanged glances, everyone bouncing telepathic thoughts from head to head, though nobody will speak up. But me.

"He's a good teacher, and this seems excessive," I say. Four says. "What's the previous conduct?"

"That is private information," says the principal. "And if he has broken a state law, that is grounds for teaching license revocation."

Well, yes, but I've had enough to drink to risk losing my head, probably a lot of people have done the same, we just had dumb luck on our side. Or we had friends around to hold us back from doing something stupid. I understand the principle, and I hate this principal.

"He doesn't deserve to be fired for one dumb mistake if he hasn't been to court yet," I say.

"He was violent," says the principal. "How can we trust he won't do that again?"

"I can trust him," says Harold.

"Me, too," I say.

"After you get your mug shot taken once, you're careful not to let it happen a second time," says Ted from across the room. He teaches algebra, is about sixty, and probably speaks from experience.

The principal frowns. He'd hoped for mass consternation.

"I wanted to make you aware of these events," he says, "and we can discuss this at a later meeting. Regardless, parents will not approve of one of our teachers being arrested for a bar fight."

"But you won't take this to the state board and ask for an investigation before he has his day in court," I say, not sure if this is a question or a command, but it sounds like the latter.

"No," he says, giving me a frown as deep as the San Andreas. I realize that everyone has been looking back and forth at us in tennis match fashion, but since I'm wearing Four, I don't care.

"Well played," Harold tells me after the staff meeting.

"He's such an ass," Ted mutters as we walk back to our rooms. "He could use a drink to loosen him up a bit."

I'm surprised to find a light on in Jack's room, though the door is closed and locked. I knock. He looks up from his desk, and walks over to let me in.

"My shit hit the fan," he says.

"I'd chew you out," I say, "but I figure your head has given you enough of a punishing."

"Don't try to teach the Revolutionary War with a hangover," he says. "My ex is talking about moving out of state, and we got into it last night. I wanted to take the edge off, but this guy was looking to pick a fight with someone. I was drinking my pint when he came along and started talking. I said some stuff, and then he gave me this shove. I shouldn't have pushed back, but he knocked over my beer. I didn't keep my cool. He was unsteady and ended up on the floor. The bartender held me back and his asshole friends called the cops. He says he twisted his ankle and hurt his wrist and some shit like that. But I'll have to hire a lawyer, and my ex has more ammo for court if I try to stop her from moving. And that asshole is after my teaching license."

"We'll fight it," I say. "All of us."

"Thanks," he says quietly.

"You're a good teacher," I say, "but don't lose your head again."

I shouldn't get so upset at other people for using the wrong head, but maybe it's because I think so much about which one I need to wear that I forget other people might not have the same awareness. And I know I don't always make the right choice. But even Four can admit that the principal is right. Regardless of whether we teachers believe Jack's story, he'll have to contend with parental opinion, which is never a tidy affair.

That night I dream I lose Four. Or maybe it rolls away. I wonder if it escaped because the other heads didn't like it much—it was a bit self-righteous and whiny, but also intelligent and determined. I sit at the kitchen table drinking coffee with Lee, wondering whether I should tell him Four is gone, because he might be upset with me. But maybe Four went to a place where it would be appreciated. Maybe it knew I didn't like having certain feelings, so it decided to get out of the picture.

When I wake up I see my open closet door and all eight heads lined up in their cubbyholes. I'm pleased and disappointed.

THINGS ARE QUIET at school for a week. I give Justin books when he starts his radiator elbow-banging, and he reads contentedly. We're not doing much group work, so Amber can keep to herself. Then I hear teachers' lounge chatter that Jack is in trouble again. Some kid punched another kid on the arm in his class, but instead of sending him down to the office, he gave the kid after-school detention in his room. When the principal heard, he called Jack down and they had more loud words.

Everyone in the teachers' lounge shakes their head. We appreciate his ethics, but Jack's mouth is going to get him in trouble.

"You're not good with PR when it comes to the principal," I say to Jack when I find him in his room after school.

"He's pretty hard to relate to," says Jack. "But geez, JDC never gets through to those kids. If I can talk to them, sometimes they give a shit. Enough to quit punching people in my class."

Nobody has gotten that physical in my classroom in a long while, but if they did...well, I'd have to think about what to do. The principal has been giving me a curt nod in the hall. I give him a curt nod back. One would feel wounded by this exchange, but Three and Seven don't care. For the staff meeting I wear Seven, which isn't as diplomatic as Three, though not as confrontational as Four.

"I have been considering the situation carefully," the principal says, "and I've decided to ask the state board of education for an investigation of Jack's assault case, following other disciplinary actions."

"What disciplinary actions?" I say.

"That is a confidential matter," says the principal.

"Then we'll write a counter letter," I say, "and sign a petition, and drive down to the state board meeting to speak for him as a good and competent teacher who's demonstrated remorse."

"I'll fit six more people in my van," says Harold.

"Four more can ride with me," says Ted.

"Jack injured another person when he was intoxicated," the principal says.

"And provoked," I say. Seven says. "Show of hands. How many people would sign a petition and drive down to Columbus to support Jack staying here?" I realize I have just taken over the meeting and this is a stupid thing to do, but I don't care. Seven doesn't care. This is the kind of behavior that killed my marriage.

Harold and Ted and twenty-odd other people raise their hands, some more slowly than others.

"How many people would support a letter to the state board asking for an investigation?" the principal says, or perhaps growls. No hands go up, but some people never raised theirs.

The principal glowers at all of us, but I'm sure his eyes fix for a moment on me.

"Given that sentiment, I will not take this matter to the state board at this time," he says slowly, "but if there are further... incidents, I may have no choice but to do so."

"Fine," I say. I cross my legs. I cross my arms. I can smell the smoke of that bridge going up in flames. Jack is a good person, the kind of guy who'd rather talk to some bully for an hour than let him go to JDC where nobody will give a shit. Harold and Ted and I don't high-five in the hall after the meeting is over, but the satisfied smirks say enough. We're willing to give the principal a war if it comes to that. Jack's one of our people. He's not.

OVER THE NEXT few weeks, when the principal sees me in the hall his stare is downright chilly, but Three or Seven can give him a smile and a nod with various amounts of sincerity. Harold greets me in the teachers' lounge with an impish grin. We all need partners in crime. I've heard that a couple of parents had meetings with Jack and the assistant principal to discuss their concerns, but there were no big waves, more like little eddies. Jack has a reputation for patience, and it seems like that's the head most parents want to imagine him wearing all the time. I think the school year might end on a calm whisper, but at the beginning of March Jack peers into my classroom and asks if we can talk for a moment. I'm not surprised when he tells me he's moving.

"It's three hours from here," he says. "I'll be closer to my parents. An hour away from my ex and my son. That won't make visitation on the weekends such a hell. And I might go back to school for my PhD. Been thinking about that for a while. I need to do something while her lawyer and my lawyer wrangle out the details."

"Okay," I say, trying to force a smile and doing a damn bad job of it. He may be able to wipe some of the tarnish off his reputation, but I'm left with this principal and my charred bridge. Should probably start my own job search. Then again, if I didn't burn bridges with the principal over Jack, something else would have sparked between him and Four or Seven soon enough. He's the kind of guy who lights fires, and those two heads aren't the sort to put them out.

"Heard Jack's going to a school with a real reputation," Harold tells me in the lounge the next day. "A couple of f-bombs won't make those kids blink. He'll get a real trial by fire, but maybe he'll be able to cool some of those kids down a bit."

"Maybe," I say, thinking about how some kids seem to use the right head all the time, and some adults never do, but the right head depends on where you are, and who's around, and what's going on. Maybe the kids at his new school have to use their street-tough heads all the time. Maybe that's how you survive. I wonder what Jack's heads will tell them. I wonder which ones he'll wear to school.

I treat head selection too much like a science, when it's not that at all. Sometimes the head I figured I should use doesn't work out, while the head I thought might lead to disaster knows just what to say. And who knows if that will work with Amber this afternoon.

I should have sent her to the office. In class today another girl asked her to take notes for their group and Amber barely wrote anything. The kid got pissed and called Amber a bitch, then Amber pinched her hard enough to leave a welt and make the girl shriek. What should have been go-to-the-office-right-now became you-have-detention-with-me-after-school.

I don't know if One likes Amber, but it wants to make sense of her. Maybe it wants to crack her shell and reveal the nice person it knows must be hiding underneath. Four and Seven think this is a load of bullshit.

I put on Four after the last bell rings, which feels good in ways it shouldn't. But why do I always have to be nice? I want to be cranky with this cranky kid and say things adults are not supposed to say, at least not to kids. I want to be contrary and truthful.

"So you hate group work," I say. "What's with that?"

"Other kids are stupid," she says, peering at the desk.

"Stupid how?"

She looks up at me, probably expected a contradiction and lecture, not another question.

"Just stupid." She sighs, like this should be obvious. "They talk too much. All they care about is who's going with who, and clothes, and makeup, and it's dumb."

"I know," I say. "I couldn't give a shit about what other people are wearing, but it's all some women think about."

She raises an eyebrow. I have her attention.

"Listen," I say, "you're doing pretty good in class on your own. You're obviously smart, just not big on group projects. I could let you be a group of one. You'd have to do more work, and maybe you'd have to stay after to get finished, but you wouldn't have to mess around with other people."

"Maybe," she says slowly, not smiling but thinking. I don't know what else to do with a kid who's on the margins and likes it there, but what's wrong with the margins? Why do we assume that people who don't play well with others must be hiding something? Why can't we figure out ways to let them be alone when they need to be?

The principal would not like this. The principal would say she has to learn to switch heads. Maybe someday, but I want her to survive my class with the head she's got.

"We can start now," I say, getting out the lab materials for the experiment she missed because I made her go to the side of the room and read after the pinching incident. She peers at the worksheet long enough to suggest she's reading it. I walk back to my desk and start grading the rest of the lab reports. Soon the only sounds in the room are the scritching of my pencil and her pen and both of our heads at work.

Athena

WHEN ATHENA SHOWS up on your doorstep it's...disturbing. You're not ready for her tirade about how your ancestor was her high priestess, and why the fuck are you working at that bank teller job? Don't you know it's a dead end and you were meant for higher things? What's become of all her temples, anyway? They're in awful disrepair if they haven't disintegrated completely.

You stare at her for a moment before stuttering that you didn't know temple upkeep and priestess-ing was supposed to be your job.

Athena says that now you do know, what are you going to do about it?

You invite her in for coffee so you can try to get your head around the situation.

The gods are real and they're sick of being ignored. Most are doing the same thing as Athena right now, finding descendants of priests to chew them out and figure out who dropped the ball.

Athena says she's going to launch a publicity campaign with you in charge. You try to remember something, anything, from the marketing class you took during your two-year stint in community college. You could make a few videos of the goddess, then put them online and hope they go viral. You could contact the media, demand interviews, and pray no one laughs at you. All of your ideas are terrifically unimpressive, but Athena says not to worry, you'll figure it out.

You wonder if Athena knows that late at night you've been lying in bed and feeling guilty for not moving up in the bank hierarchy. You've told people the job is temporary, but you're not sure what you want to be permanent. At family functions you explain to aunts and uncles and cousins that you plan on going back to school, but most of them don't believe you anymore. Marketing a goddess wasn't one of the career options you'd considered, but it doesn't seem worse than the job you have at present.

Flipping through the news channels, you realize the whole world is having a problem getting their heads around this one. Poseidon is on anti-whaling ships attacking whale-hunting vessels. Demeter is working with environmental activists on campaigns to stop pollution. Zeus is on all the nightly news shows trying to account for inclement weather—hurricanes and tornadoes and typhoons. He explains he was just trying to get everyone's attention, but it didn't work as well as he'd hoped.

"We realized a media campaign was the only way," says Athena, speaking for herself and the rest of the gods. They just didn't expect such a skeptical world, assumed everyone would believe what they saw on TV. A huge chunk of the population has become wary of everything, however, and is too jaded to believe this.

Some groups say the appearance of the gods is part of a right-wing conspiracy. Others says it's a left-wing conspiracy. Various commentators with political agendas say it's a sign of the second coming, while others repeat that these "gods" are aliens. A few scientists postulate that in some parallel universes no one ever stopped believing in the gods, so your world is just falling in line with them.

But none of that matters right now because you need to launch a world tour and help Athena become computer literate. At least she's a fast learner. She also likes fried chicken, french fries, fried shrimp, and fried pies. Happily she's immortal and her cholesterol level doesn't matter, because you need to order a lot of takeout—there's no time for cooking.

Soon your living room is command central and her shrine. After word about the goddess gets out on Internet bulletin boards and blogs, crowds can't be stopped. People come to your door with questions and buckets of fried chicken and biscuits to give her as an offering. Athena looks thoughtful while she eats and dispenses advice. Most of her supplicants seem to need career counseling, so she doles out aptitude tests along with job applications for her publicity campaign. You're not a priestess, you're a campaign manager. Same difference, Athena tells you. She's running for credibility.

While most of her worshippers are very nice, you don't appreciate her setting naysayers and other belligerent people on fire in your living room. It chars the carpet and leaves an awful black spot, but at least she looks embarrassed and buys you a nice throw rug to cover up the dark bits. You never liked your carpet much, so it's an improvement.

In the evening you watch Zeus on TV apologizing for the awful nor'easter that just hit the coast. He doesn't sweat in his suit and tie, just says if people stopped and listened to him he wouldn't do things like that.

Athena rolls her eyes and mutters over her father's tendency to act first and think later.

The next week she invites him to your place for beer, pizza, and cheesecake. He sits beside you on the couch and rests his hand on your knee. Athena lounges in an armchair and says her priestess is off limits.

Zeus takes his hand from your knee but gives you a wink. He's cute and charismatic for an older guy. You've only admitted that about Richard Gere and Harrison Ford before, and they can't shape-shift into cats. Zeus knows you like longhairs and becomes an orange tabby who winds around your legs when his daughter is out of the room. You reach down and scratch him between the ears. He purrs. You feel like this is the kind of cat you could keep forever, one that could sleep on your bed, one that could sleep *in* your bed.

The evening is interrupted by another news story that makes Zeus turn back into his human form and Athena race from the bathroom, still zipping the fly on her jeans. Poseidon sent a sea monster to destroy a whaling ship, and there were human casualties. Now he's having a press conference and is alternately defensive and apologetic, saying he warned them he'd do something drastic if they didn't leave the whales alone.

"Shit," comments Athena. "He can be such an ass." But all the gods are surprised at the public reaction to their presence. They won obedience so easily before and sank ships all the time. Nobody demanded an explanation back then.

Athena wants to tackle the morning talk shows to gain new devotees, and she asks you to contact the Defense Department and set up a meeting so she can let them know what they're doing right and what they're doing wrong. When you balk she says she plans to use more tact than other members of her family.

"You win more flies with honey than vinegar," she says with a wink. "It rarely helps to simply tell people how they screwed up, even if it's mostly true."

Athena doesn't tell you how you screwed up, just how you could do things better. When you give her control of your small stock portfolio, she reinvests everything and it doubles in value in a week. You quit your job, which she says you should have done a long time ago, but you hadn't used up all your sick leave before now.

When her brother Apollo comes over for fried chicken and ice cream sundaes, you develop a massive crush and barely eat anything at dinner because he keeps giving you flirty glances across the table. Your heart is a sweet melty ice cream puddle, but after he leaves, Athena pats your shoulder and says to save your affection for someone else. All the male gods are love 'em and leave 'em types, and you don't have time for that kind of drama.

You launch her world tour with a band. It's half rock concert and half political campaign, complete with loud music and flashing lights and speeches by prominent Hollywood supporters, then Athena's own speech, which runs a half hour. She's an excellent speaker, very funny and engaging, and she tells great stories. She ends the evening by saying she's accessible through e-mails, tweets, and burnt offerings, she especially likes chocolate fried pies and fried chicken, and she can bless your wedding or career or soldier wife before she goes off to war.

You run yourself ragged behind the scenes coordinating sound and lighting and the speakers, wrapped up in the frantic adrenaline rush of being a promoter. Even when you get the flu for a week and feel like shit, you don't want to stop working. After Athena does something weird to your head that makes you less congested, you keep plugging ahead. You can't stop moving, you're part of something huge. Customer service at the bank was never like this.

To your surprise, the Defense Department takes your call seriously. At the end of the world tour, you jet off with Athena as her personal assistant and high priestess, keeper of the scheduling book and sacred briefcase. You're becoming a little overzealous about telling supporters where you and Athena will head next, but you enjoy the adoring mob that follows you everywhere and how you can pretend you're a rock star.

When a masked whacko shoots at you both as you're standing on a sidewalk outside the Capitol, Athena rips off your blouse and performs emergency surgery on your chest to extract the bullet that lodged inches away from your heart. Her quick thinking yanks you from the moving sidewalk of the underworld back into reality.

When your vital signs are stable and she's staunched the flow of blood, she chases down the gunman and rips out his lungs. Literally. Then she calls the police.

Ten minutes later, four guys with badges stand around gaping at the mangled gunman's body and decide to call her act self-defense. They were pretty sure he had a gun aimed at Athena, or at least witnesses can be convinced to report that was the case.

YOU GET HOME and find your on-again off-again boyfriend has left eight messages on your answering machine. He wants to be on-again, but you're wise to that line. Things are going well for you, your career, and your stock portfolio. He broke it off six months ago to "see other people" and you haven't heard much from him since, but your bed has become a lot more attractive now. You gleefully delete his whines. If he wants to bring you offerings of chocolate, maybe you'll consider having dinner with him, but if you fall for anyone now it'll be Apollo or Hermes, who visits Athena's shrine/your living room regularly. He has a motorcycle, which he says has more style than the old winged sandals.

You usually don't go for men in black leather, but make an exception for Hermes. While Athena is out getting coffee with Aphrodite, Hermes swings by and asks if you want to go for pizza. You need a break from replying to the thousands of e-mails, so you say sure. He whisks you off on the back of his bike, which leads not only to pizza, but beer and jokes heavy with innuendo and sharing a pint of mint chocolate chip ice cream on your couch.

You've never believed in one-night stands, but that doesn't stop you from waking up naked in bed with Hermes looking sheepish, and your goddess boss standing over you and tapping her foot on your bedroom floor. You cower back under the sheets and wonder if she's going to smite you, but she's more upset with Hermes.

"My priestess is off limits," she says. "Can't you control yourself for one night? We don't need complications like this."

You tell her it's okay, you're on the pill, but she says it doesn't matter. Gods have very insistent sperm.

You swallow hard.

"You'll be here every night and give her a foot massage," Athena says to Hermes, "and of course there will be regular visits and child support payments after that."

He nods. You feel light-headed.

Your crash course in giving birth to a divine being lasts a month. All you want to eat is peanut butter on toast and mashed potatoes with a lot of butter. You get the worst headaches ever as your stomach inflates into a basketball. You cradle it in a sling for extra support. Hermes visits every day as promised to bring you ice cream, give you foot massages, and ask how you're feeling. You know Athena would be royally pissed if he weren't attentive. He kisses you on the cheek, not the lips, when he leaves. You resign yourself to the fact that this won't be a forever romance.

During your month of pregnancy, you work at home on the computer and phone. Staying seated is a good idea since you're a little spacey from whatever Athena did to take your headaches and horrible morning sickness away. You're concerned because you've done research since you got pregnant, and read all the myths about mortals giving birth to immortals. Not all of them survive when the baby wants to come out. Athena grits her teeth and says you'll be fine.

YOU LIE ON your bed screaming. The kid feels like she's going to rip you in half.

Athena snaps her fingers and takes you out of your body. Floating above the bed, you wonder absently if you died. You give birth to a little girl who looks like a perfectly normal pink baby except for the wings on her heels. She's already in your arms wrapped in a lavender blanket when Athena slides you back into your skin, though you still feel floaty.

Hermes comes over the next day with a plush octopus for his new daughter and flowers and chocolate for you. He smiles, waggles his fingers at the infant, and says he wants to take her to Olympus and show her off to the rest of the gods.

"Fuck no," says Athena. "She's staying with us."

He grumbles but later brings the baby Pegasus toys and boxes and boxes of diapers. Your new daughter levitates while nursing, and she eats a lot. At least your hands are free so you can keep returning e-mails and phone calls, but a day later you fall into some weird form of postpartum depression. Hermes gives you fleeting kisses on the cheek when he arrives and when he leaves. You feel like you've become another myth, a footnote in a long list of nymphs and maidens he had kids with. Nothing special. How could you let yourself fall so easily into temptation, even cute temptation wearing black leather and riding a motor-cycle? You're a slut.

Athena rolls her eyes and says to quit moping and get over yourself. You're not cheap or loose, you're her campaign manager and high priestess and you still have duties to attend to.

"The kid can come on the road with us when she's old enough," says Athena. "Divine ones age at different rates so who knows how long that will be, but we have plenty to keep us busy until then."

Athena grabs a bucket of fried chicken from her latest sup-plicant and hands you a drumstick. You eat as your floating baby nurses and your boss twirls a pen between her fingers, what she usually does during brainstorming sessions.

You soon discover that having a child with a god has deep-ened your involvement in the pantheon, since your daughter has a slew of immortal aunties and uncles who often drop by to visit. The first time Aphrodite comes over to babysit you're rather taken aback, but Athena says not to worry, she's great with kids and you need time to have dinner together and discuss her cur-rent campaign strategy. It's only when you slide into her car that you realize you're totally exhausted. You need to relax and have a drink.

The maternal separation anxiety is strange at first, but you relax a little after the hors d'oeuvres (since Athena said you had to order the fried ravioli). Your kid will have twenty divine aun-ties cooing over her at all times, so as long as Hermes remembers his manners and doesn't bring over any nymph girlfriends, everything should be okay. Most working mothers don't have it nearly this good.

Before your lasagna arrives, Athena gets down to business. She needs help with her Facebook account, and advice on managing a nasty line of tweets from some dickhead in Poughkeepsie. She'd like to smite him with fire, but knows that would be bad PR.

"What about turning him into a panda bear?" she says. "Everyone loves panda bears and they're endangered, so that would add another one to the list."

You nod slowly and, like a good campaign manager priestess, begin to consider how you might spin this one to the nightly news shows.

In the Dim Below

THIS HAD BEEN the routine since I was born, bombs coming every few years, or every few months, whenever there was another reason for everyone on one side of the river to get mad at everyone on the other side of the river, or vice versa. The sirens blew and we had to go inside, or down below, until the blasts stopped, the smoke mostly cleared, and we could come up and see what was left of the world.

It was bad when you were a kid. Bombs had no eyes to make decisions, couldn't tell soldiers from children. Each of us had seen at least one friend's body carried from a pile of stone that had once been a house. Our parents told us not to worry because they were shooting bombs back across the river to keep us safe. We didn't know how that was supposed to stop the other bombs, or why faceless enemies imagined us as soldiers instead of friends. Didn't they have kids on the other side of the river, kids who looked something like us? But we couldn't ask questions, we just had to find a tiny space where bombs could not find us.

That's what we were trying to do on the day a hole appeared in Amina's front yard. It was not smoking. It was not smelly. It was five feet wide and a perfect circle, with grass growing down, down, down into the dark. It didn't make sense, how the grass could be so lush in a hole so deep. We took turns poking our heads inside, sitting in the hole like it was a huge slide we were afraid to go down. What could be waiting at the end? A burrow of bunnies, or rabid badgers, or something else entirely? No one wanted to guess.

The next round of bombs came before dinner and everyone went to their basements again, ready for the world to rumble and break off in pieces. We were ready for more children wrapped in white cloth, ready for parades through the streets with bodies borne on tears. We were not ready for the wail of Amina's mother. Where had her daughter gone?

But we found her ten minutes after the bombing, standing in her yard. She had crawled into the hole, slid to a space where there was no rumbling, where the world was dark and safe.

Amina's mother hugged her. She didn't notice what I saw, how a small thing was missing, the index finger on Amina's left hand. Amina only showed us, her friends, when her mother had gone back inside and I grabbed her arm.

"I'll be fine," Amina told us with a strange calm. "I lost my finger in the hole, but I don't remember how...It didn't hurt." There was no blood, no nub, just three fingers, smooth skin, and a thumb.

"How do you know you'll be okay?" I asked.

"I just do," she said with a shrug.

The next time bombs came Amina was not in the basement, she was in her house. The blast blew a hole through her concrete living room wall, but we found Amina sitting in the clearing smoke cloud without a scratch. She wasn't even coughing.

"My miracle girl," her mother wailed, hugging Amina close. "Never do that again! You must have been protected by angels."

Amina smiled at us from her mother's embrace, wriggling the four digits on her left hand.

WHAT WOULD YOU give up to be safe?

86

That was a game we played, wagering favorite toys and even our homes, never pets or parents or siblings, even if a bratty brother or sister came to mind. There was a lot we would give up for that nod from the angels, a promise to shield us from shrapnel.

That's why we started to think about the hole in Amina's front yard.

Her mother and our parents and the rest of the adult world figured it was a bomb blast, but they were busy with adult lives, didn't think to look at it more closely.

Four days after the bomb hit Amina's house, Ravvi bit his lower lip and nodded.

"I'll try it," he said. We sat around the hole as he slid down. I held my breath, fingers crossed, picking blades of grass one by one and weaving them into rings. Three minutes. Six minutes. Nine minutes later, Ravvi crawled out on his elbows, blinking into the sun, without an index finger on his left hand. He winced a little when we touched the absence.

"That's normal," said Amina, who was now our expert on the hole. "My hand hurt for a little bit and then it went away. Once you figure out how to do things with three fingers and a thumb, it's fine."

The next bombing was that afternoon. We scurried to basements. Amina and Ravvi were playing in her yard when a missile hit next door, and they didn't stop the game of catch just because of smoke and flying glass. When we heard Amina's mother scream, we thought something awful had happened, but it was the opposite.

"You can't depend on miracles," she yelled, bending over her daughter and ready to slap her, but Amina gave her a sweet dream gaze that stopped her mother's hand.

"Remember the angels," Amina said, though I knew it wasn't angels but something else. After that, more of our friends were willing to slide down the grass. They told the same story when they came up—after they couldn't see light from above, everything became hazy and unclear. They felt a shove from behind, found themselves turned around and climbing out of the hole on grass-stained knees, back into the light. They couldn't remember losing the finger, and smiled peacefully.

"It's like I know the bombs won't be able to touch me," said my friend Hanna. "Like everything will be fine."

Going into that hole made them immune from something larger and darker, a logical wartime equation. Losing a finger was easier than losing a hand or foot or arm or leg or many other more precious things. But I was nervous to climb down it myself.

"It can't be that bad," Amina told me.

I nodded, still not convinced, though no one screamed or yelped or made any kind of noise when they were in the hole. We listened closely, three or four of us sticking our heads inside. Before now we had always been scared, tensed to run to safe places that did not exist. But when their houses were destroyed, everyone who had crawled into that hole was safe, without a scratch, even if they had broken glass on their skin. The adults said it was angels and we were blessed children. We knew better.

MY FRIENDS SAID I should do it to protect myself.

"We'll worry about you if you don't," said Amina, but I tucked my hands behind my body, scared of whatever lion or snake would bite my finger off, even if it would fill me with magic venom.

But Amina told other kids, and soon ten of them had gone down into the hole. Our parents were too busy launching bombs over the river to notice missing fingers. There was too much else on their minds. Once the bombs were supposed to stop for four hours so people could go shopping, but the bombs came over the river anyway. Ravvi was at the market.

"It was awful," he said with a shudder, but he and his brother who'd gone into the hole were fine. Soon we'd have a town composed only of kids missing a finger, kids who'd want to be soldiers and send more bombs over the river. If I went into the hole, maybe I'd be tempted to stay there forever, in the dark that no one remembered.

But then something stranger happened. When Beena came up she was missing two fingers from her left hand. She blinked and shrugged and said it was okay, she could still write. Her brother had been killed the previous week in the market. Two fingers was a fair trade. She had to stay alive for her parents, willing to pay for safety though the price had gone up.

But I was more afraid, drowning in worry and what if's. What if someday a kid didn't come back up? What if the creature in the hole upped the price to a foot or a hand? What was it doing with all those fingers anyway?

Three days later, a bomb fell on my best friend Linna's house and her leg was crushed by granite blocks. Doctors did what they could to help her, but the hospital had been hit three times. I knew she wouldn't walk again. I took a deep breath, ready for the hole.

THE GRASS WAS soft and warm, though I shivered a little. I was scared to go, but more scared not to go, barefoot as always because I ran around without sandals. My mother said the soles of my feet were hard as rock. Later I had waking dreams of what happened—spirits taking my hands and feet in their warm grasp, kissing my palms and breathing into them, light filling my body like blood, bright and sharp as a blade. I cried out, but was turned around and crawling out of the hole. When I emerged, blinking into the light, I found I had paid a greater price. I'd lost a finger from each hand, a baby toe from each foot, but even worse was what I had gained. Sadness like a weight in my mind, my heart.

Everyone else had been filled with peace, with ease, with joy, but all I wanted to do was cry on the couch. I was not hungry or thirsty. I was looking out the window and waiting for the next bomb, the next light trail. My parents couldn't stop me when I tore out of their grasp, out of the house. I ran toward the bombs, picturing the rubble, the kids I could save, wondering who might be lying on the ground this time. I carried a lunchbox with alcohol wipes and Band-Aids and gauze, ready to hug other kids as they trembled, to whisper to them about the hole, to show them what I had sacrificed, to tell them it was worth it.

Broken glass didn't cut my feet. Concrete didn't scrape my arms. I might have felt pain sometimes, but I had to get to people under the rubble. My friends didn't come with me at first, but then one day I was playing kickball with Ravvi and we heard a bomb streaking across the sky. I grabbed his hand and he ran with me without resisting. We waded into the smoke, cleared away stones, looked for people who had survived, cut and shaken but still breathing.

We were not scared.

"What are you doing?" adults yelled. "This is too dangerous for children! Go back home." But our homes had turned to piles of stone. I gave the adults a hard stare. It was no place for them, either, but we all had to save who we could, because that was the only thing to do.

I hoped there was another hole on the other side of the river. I hoped there were more kids losing small pieces of themselves so they could live through the bombs. Maybe someday there'd be a bridge across the river and we'd be older and could meet them, the kids-turned-adults, who we'd know because they were like us, missing a finger or a toe, their eyes tired and relieved as we met in the middle, over the water, and embraced.

For now I dreamed myself standing in the middle of a field, a missile rocketing toward me, but I caught it and held it in my arms, and it shivered like a scared animal, one that didn't know how to do anything but fight. I stroked its head, the coarse fur, and placed it gently on the ground. It had become something like a badger, harmless and confused, and walked away. I waited to catch the next one I knew would be coming.

The Hero

HE LOOKED PAINFULLY normal until one noticed his seven fingers and very large shoes and habit of standing quietly with his hands behind his back during staff meetings at the appliance store where he did inventory and bookkeeping. Most people assumed his silence meant he was shy instead of brilliant, but he was a super-genius and super-strong and lived in fear that anyone would find out. He reasoned every hero needed a villain nemesis to counteract his power, and he didn't see the point. They'd end up fighting and canceling each other out when it would be much easier to forget the whole thing and go out for a beer. In the name of efficiency and conservation of time and drama, he was determined to save the world by doing nothing. The more a hero did, he reasoned, the more the world would need saving. That's just how super-smart he was.

Like many heroes he was an orphan. His parents had been killed when he was a baby and a blimp advertising athletic footwear rammed into their house. The accident propelled his infant carrier into the low branches of a pine tree, where it was found by an old woman who drove the elementary school bus. She carried him to her cabin and spoon-fed him goat's milk mixed with honey and espresso. Even then she knew he would be a special child who could chop all the wood they needed for the winter in one afternoon and drag her two-wheel-drive Gremlin out of snowbanks.

The hero grew tall and strong and seriously addicted to caffeine. Every morning at breakfast his foster mother told him the gossip from town, as she was a seer and could glance at people and know who they really were. She cheerily informed him that the man who managed the corner gas station had royal French blood and was the lover of the high school band director, the waitress at the Italian restaurant downtown had just become pregnant with identical twins courtesy of a shoe store salesman, and the bank vice president had a foot fetish and was screwing his secretary while worshiping her toes.

Her foster son smiled and added two teaspoons of sugar to his coffee. He didn't care much for his mother's gossip, but knew she needed to tell someone because her gift of seeing wasn't much fun unless she could divulge everyone's secrets. After his mother poured her second cup of coffee, she checked him for bumps and bruises that she knew would indicate wounds he'd receive during the day. She found a tiny divot in his finger that suggested he'd get a paper cut, but nothing more serious.

The hero didn't have his own car, so his mother drove him to work in her Gremlin. He spent the day tucked in a small office behind a fortress of paper where he clicked his fingers across a calculator. He loved the logic of numbers and how they sat in even rows, and he loved how his job meant he didn't have to talk with anyone for most of the day. The hero was especially fearful of talking to women, since they were drawn to him in a way he didn't understand. Most of them didn't understand it either, but that didn't stop ladies from swooning when he ordered a double espresso at the local coffee shop. It was a bit of a pain since he had to pick them up off the floor and prop them in chairs so nobody would step on them before the women came to, but by the time he was finished the barista had extracted his espresso. He gave her an extra tip for cluttering the floor.

He knew women only meant trouble for heroes, since any of his lovers would be endangered by the super-villains he was trying so hard not to attract. The helpless lady would be captured or otherwise put in jeopardy, and he'd have to take off work for a few hours to save her, which he'd do in the nick of time, and afterwards she'd cling to him and pledge her eternal love and require years of therapy to come to grips with the experience. As with many other things in his life, he knew the script and figured it wasn't worth the hassle.

While the hero ran sweet rows of numbers through his calculator he wondered if it wouldn't be easier to build a cabin in the middle of nowhere and telecommute to work. It would only take him half a day to string the necessary cables and rig up a high-speed Internet connection, and he worried if he didn't do it soon then someone would discover his superpowers and he'd need to save the world by destroying a meteorite or moving the whole damn planet for one reason or another and then putting it back in the right spot, which probably wouldn't be easy, and who wanted to be responsible for all that?

The only thing that stopped him from relocating to the hassle-free middle of nowhere was the barista who worked at the coffee shop he frequented on his lunch break. She was the only woman who managed not to swoon when he spoke, and he loved watching her hands as she measured out the right amount of ground espresso beans and tamped them down and extracted the thick liquid into a tiny cup and asked him for two-fifty. She didn't take his order anymore, just started the drink when she saw him walk into the shop.

The hero was terribly worried that she'd turn out to be evil since she wore all black and very thick eyeshadow and had that curious habit of not swooning when he spoke. It would be a shame if she tried to take over the world and he had to destroy her (a word that sounded far more noble than "kill" even though he admitted it was the same thing). He wanted to ask her out on a date, but knew that would endanger his or her life in some way.

At the coffee shop he sat at a table next to the cash register and glanced at her just often enough for her to ask if he wanted another double shot. He shook his head, knowing the way she smiled at him was suspect. There was something insidious in the way her lips curled upwards. He moped back to the appliance store, moped out to the parking lot when his mother came to pick him up from work, and moped as he made four-cheese lasagna for dinner.

While they ate, his mother asked what was wrong.

"Nothing," the hero said in a way that suggested everything was wrong.

"You should ask her to a movie," said his mother.

He shook his head, knew the movie theater would blow up halfway through the film and he'd never get to see the end.

The next day, however, he decided to see if the coffee shop girl wanted to go out for lunch. Not asking was driving him crazy, and after she said yes he could decide whether he wanted to go through with it or build his cabin in the mountains. He didn't figure the world would be in serious danger until they were in close proximity during their lunch date.

After she handed him the double espresso, he smiled and said he'd love to get lunch with her the next day. She smiled that small insidious smile.

"I'm sorry," she said. "That's sweet, but I have a boyfriend."

"Oh," he said before taking his usual seat and gritting his teeth. Her boyfriend was probably evil, likely the person meant to be his nemesis. The hero stayed at the coffee shop longer than usual, past the end of his lunch break, hoping to see Evil Boyfriend. He knew he'd be able to make a decent excuse to his boss for his tardiness, and the lie could be forgiven since the fate of the world might very well be at stake.

When the seven-foot-tall man lumbered into the coffee shop, the hero knew it was the barista's Evil Boyfriend even before she pecked a kiss on his cheek. The giant was slim, had dark hair, and wore a shy grin to conceal the fact that he walked around crushing steel cans with two fingers. Naturally the lovers had been sent to plot against the hero, so he needed to reveal their evil plan or build a cabin in the woods in short order.

When Evil Boyfriend left the coffee shop with his double mocha with whipped cream, the hero followed him two blocks to a record store. Since he'd already overshot his lunch break by an hour, the hero figured waiting a bit longer to return to work wouldn't make much difference. He perused the aisles while using his keen sight to monitor the giant Evil Boyfriend working the register. Over two hours the hero failed to uncover any plots or even any unnecessary expletives, though he knew evil had to be tucked away somewhere.

The hero walked back to the appliance store and explained to his boss that he'd been violently ill in a bathroom for two hours. His boss grimaced and asked why he'd been spotted an hour ago in the record store. The hero glanced at his feet, unable to explain his true goals of saving the world from destruction, and muttered that he'd been looking for a birthday gift for his mother. His boss said that if personal matters ever detained him again, they'd need to have A Serious Talk. The hero said he understood and tucked himself in the back room to ponder how he should save the coffee shop girl from her Evil Boyfriend, but that proved difficult since he didn't know Evil Boyfriend's true intentions.

The following day was Saturday, so he borrowed his mother's car and drove into town to get his nails done. The hero liked his hands to look good since he had seven fingers, and he especially liked his manicurist. She was four feet tall, had purple hair and five piercings in each ear, and walked so fast it looked like her feet didn't touch the ground. When she wore a tank top he could see small wings tattooed on her back. She knew he had seven fingers and she knew he was super-strong and could open any impossible bottle of nail polish, but she was not impressed. He appreciated that.

Sometimes the hero wasn't sure how much he should trust his manicurist, but once he sat down in her blue chair he ended up telling her too much about his personal life. He wondered if she was an enchantress and the salon was under a truth-telling spell, but it could have just been the overwhelming chemical odor of nail polish and solvents that loosened everyone's tongues. Regardless of the cause, she was never surprised when he unloaded his emotions.

"Maybe I should take off work for two days and follow the boyfriend around town," the hero said. "Or maybe I should make all my girlfriends sign a contract so I won't be held liable if misfortune befalls them." He'd never had a girlfriend, but that was beside the point.

"You're such a dork," said his manicurist. "You need to save the world from your big head more than you need to save it from a meteor."

The hero frowned. "You never know when a meteor might pop up and need to be destroyed."

"Hold still while I'm polishing," she said.

He pouted quietly, then said, "I know I have a big head. I needed the largest hat when I was in high school marching band."

"It hasn't shrunk since," she said.

The hero sulked all the way home, figured that when the meteor came he wouldn't save the world after all and see how she liked that. To distract himself he spent the afternoon building a two-story treehouse with electrical wiring and plumbing, then he made two dozen cheesecakes and sent one to his manicurist because he'd given her a shitty tip and wanted to make up for it.

On Monday morning when he walked to the coffee shop, things were no better. When he saw the barista he felt a surge of dragonflies coursing through his body. He wanted to grab her and rip off her clothes and make mythic love to her on the table next to the cash register, but he knew she might become pregnant with a kid who'd rend her body in half. In the evening he muttered his laments to his mother, who said it was normal hero libido and to take a cold shower.

On Tuesday morning when his mother felt his body she noted a disturbing bump on his knee. She said it wouldn't be fatal but probably painful, and she didn't know how he'd get it.

"Probably on a chair or something," she said as they drove to work. "Just be careful."

She dropped him off behind the appliance store, but he found the door was locked. When he walked around to the front he saw all seven other employees milling around the parking lot as a police officer explained that the store was being shut down for tax evasion. The owner hadn't filed her taxes for the past ten years, concealing all store profits from the government, so the inventory was being confiscated to sell at auction.

The hero felt like his body had turned to stone. He'd done all the taxes and given the forms to his boss to review and sign and send in. She'd always been nice to him and the other employees, gave them large holiday bonuses and cakes on their birthdays and even a free microwave when he told her his mother's twenty-year-old model had just died.

The hero shook his head and made blood pump back into his granite legs so he could walk to the building and lean against the wall. He was embarrassed that he hadn't apprehended Evil Boss, but she'd seemed so kind.

He glanced at the policemen and seven other employees, expecting to see them glare since he hadn't saved the store from imminent danger, but nobody seemed to blame him for the closing or even give him a second glance.

They were all without jobs, and he knew his coworkers had spouses and children to support. They were making phone calls to friends and family and prospective new employers, pitching themselves and their sales abilities and their twenty years in the business. The hero had only ever worked at the appliance store, and had no idea where to start looking for a new job.

He could build that cabin and live in the mountains like he'd been planning to do for years, but now that the idea was a real option he didn't like it as much. It sounded boring and lonely, because even though he didn't talk to many people, he didn't like the idea of not seeing anyone for days. He also didn't want to end up a grown child living with his mother and being supported by her paycheck. He could do odd jobs for the neighbors—mowing lawns and chopping wood and moving their garages ten feet to the left—but he knew that wouldn't be enough.

For a full half minute he pouted, mad that his mother hadn't foretold this event, hadn't seen his boss was the evil person he should defeat. His mother was more interested in using her abilities to divulge steamy affairs, though he admitted there was rarely any other secret knowledge in town worth knowing.

The hero glanced at his coworkers, who were still on their cell phones and did not appear to need saving. He left them in the parking lot negotiating new lives and walked to the coffee shop for his usual double espresso, hoping it would make him think more clearly. On the way there he realized his fatal flaw. All heroes had one, of course, and he'd thought his was caffeine, but now he realized it was something more.

He was super-smart, but only in a logical way. He wasn't good at reading people, selling things, or figuring out what a customer needed to hear. He wasn't an entrepreneur. Last year when he'd tried to sell a washing machine by explaining how well it could get bloodstains out of denim, he'd driven the customers out of the store in two minutes flat.

The hero moped into the coffee shop and sat at his usual table with his double espresso.

"What's wrong?" said the coffee shop girl. He glanced at her and noted she'd painted her nails dark purple, but he didn't care to consider whether or not this was more evidence of her true nature.

"I just lost my job," he said. "It turned out that my boss was evil."

The coffee shop girl screwed her face into a frown. "Can you make espresso and lattes and things like that? Somebody on my shift just quit, so we're down an employee."

He stood up so fast that he banged his knee on the table. It really smarted, but he didn't care as he bounded over the counter. She gave him a lesson in how to grind espresso beans and tamp them down and extract the brew. The hero was good at being precise and following directions, so soon he was whipping out drinks at three times the speed of any other employee. When the coffee shop girl asked him to tidy the eating area, the tables and chairs shone like gold in five minutes.

After working two eight-hour shifts, the hero had filled the tip jar and wasn't even tired. The coffee shop girl invited him to come out to the bar with her and her boyfriend to celebrate his first day on the job.

"I swear, we should have hired you years ago," she said as she walked arm in arm with Evil Boyfriend. "You make the best lattes ever."

The hero smiled, momentarily willing to overlook that the girl and her boyfriend were evil. At the bar they bought him two beers, then he bought a pitcher because he couldn't feel the alcohol and assumed it was weak. By the end of the night he was doing shots of tequila from a pint glass.

Twelve hours later he woke up on the coffee shop girl's couch with the biggest hangover ever. It would have killed anyone who wasn't a hero, but as it was he felt pretty damn bad. The coffee shop girl smiled at him as she tottered into the living room.

"You fucking drank everyone else under the table," she said. "Do you feel like having breakfast?"

While the hero's head was pounding with the force of ten thousand horses, he was always hungry in the morning. Evil Boyfriend had already gone out for bagels, and while they waited for him to come back, the hero helped the coffee shop girl get out plates and butter and jam. Evil Boyfriend returned with the bagels, and before he knew it the hero was sitting at the kitchen table with them having breakfast. He realized this situation could quickly lead to the destruction of the world, and he needed to let the coffee shop girl and Evil Boyfriend know he was on to their plans so they'd better not try anything. It would require a more direct approach than he'd wanted to use, but he knew there were no other options.

"Have you ever considered doing anything evil?" he said as he buttered his bagel.

"I want to ship the neighbor's dog to Anchorage," said the coffee shop girl. "It's so damn yappy and sometimes it doesn't shut up until two in the morning. I guess you didn't hear it last night since you were tanked."

"No," the hero said, "I mean really evil."

"Once I tried to flush a cherry bomb down the high school toilet but it didn't work," Evil Boyfriend said. "The toilet just over-flowed."

"When I was eight I took half of my sister's Halloween candy," said the coffee shop girl, "but then she found out and got mad and my mom made me pay her back for it."

"There was the time in fourth grade when I teased the fat girl on the playground," said Evil Boyfriend, "but then in high school she slimmed down and did weight training and now she's a model in New York and makes millions of dollars and half the guys in my graduating class would probably be honored to have her spit on them in the street."

"Oh," said the hero as he ate half his bagel in one bite and the coffee shop girl and Evil Boyfriend turned the discussion to what they should make for dinner that night. They decided ravi-oli would be a good idea.

At the coffee shop the hero made four lattes a minute and felt terribly depressed. What if there wasn't enough real evil in the world, at least not the lightning-bolt-throwing tidal-wave-machine-constructing bent-on-world-dominion-through-zombie-army kind of evil he knew he could combat? What if there were more people avoiding their taxes and shutting down businesses and putting other people out of work? What the hell was he sup-posed to do about crooked accountants? How was he supposed to find them and hack into their computers and donate all their profits to charities for poor children and abandoned animals?

It was too awful to conceive. He'd lived his life thinking that he was in danger of putting the world in danger if anyone found out about his abilities, but what if it wasn't true? That's what he lamented to his manicurist during his next appointment. She said he needed a good drink. He said he'd tried that already. She said he obviously hadn't tried the right drink and they should go out after she got off work.

They got Italian food at a small family-run restaurant with big portions and reasonably good wine. He had three helpings of lasagna, then she took him back to her place for chocolate cookies and more wine, which led to her slowly undressing him to examine his seven toes.

"You need a pedicure," she said before she took control of his heroic male parts. He'd never had sex before and wasn't accustomed to the head-swirling sensations.

"Wow," he said afterwards.

"That was okay," she said, propping herself up on one elbow and smiling at him.

"Just okay?" he said.

"It's the sort of thing where you get better with practice," she said. "You have to learn what your partner likes."

"I didn't get it right?" he said.

"You did okay," she said, "but your ego is getting in the way again. I'd rather concentrate on other parts of your body."

"Oh," he said, falling back against the pillow. All heroes were supposed to be masters of romance.

White as Soap

I'M NOT SURE what to think when the people from the soap company call and ask about filming a commercial at my unicorn ranch. They want to feature unicorns wild and free and running across the open prairie and all that other romantic shit.

"Unicorns have a great universal appeal," says the director. "They're mythic and romantic. That's the sort of thing that will sell soap."

"Oh," I say because I sell unicorns and not soap. After raising unicorns for twenty years I've learned that there is nothing romantic about them. I also have a vague notion that doing a commercial could be classified as selling out, but I've also been told that the kind of people who talk about "selling out" are the kind of people who can't sell anything. What matters is if you can live with yourself in the morning.

I'm not worried about being able to live with myself, as my primary morning concern is if the unicorns will get fed, not only on that morning but on subsequent mornings. People aren't buying unicorns like they used to. They're considered a luxury item, even though I argue strongly against that idea. Most people overlook the practical uses of unicorns as work animals—a unicorn is no more expensive than a good horse, and just as strong. Unicorn owners and breeders simply have to be aware of unicorn biology and certain medical concerns like horn rot. But I digress.

In the end it comes down to having more food for the blessing versus less food for the blessing, so I say yes. The director says she and a camera crew will be out in two weeks. She doesn't sound pleased when I tell her that the nearest airport is four hours away, but this is Wyoming so what do you expect?

I say she and her crew should schedule three days to be around before they start shooting.

"Do you really need three days?" she says.

"It takes the unicorns a while to get used to new people," I say. "Some of them will be curious and some will be scared." By the time the camera crew arrives I will have selected the unis that would be good candidates for the commercial, but I'll need to see their reactions to the crew and their equipment to be certain.

The director agrees but sounds a bit grudging about it.

"These are domesticated unicorns," I say, "but they're not used to cameras. If you need trained unis, I can tell you who to call." I've sold a few unicorns to wranglers who train animals for the movies. I've saddle-broken a few of my unis, but I don't have time for much beyond that.

The director says she wants to use the "wild backdrop" of Wyoming and so my untrained unis will be fine. I figure she's probably working on the cheap and doesn't want to shoulder the cost of more expensive animals and handlers.

She says she'll get my contract and all the necessary forms in the mail to me this afternoon.

I explain the arrangement to my ranch hand Orrin when we eat lunch in the farmhouse. He nods like he's not excited about the idea. I'm not surprised at his reaction, but pretend that I am.

"What's wrong?" I say.

"Nothing."

"You're worried."

"They don't like it when a lot of strangers come around," he says. "They get moody. It's a hell of a lot harder to keep them

103

under control."

"That's why I'm having everyone in the crew come early."

"I hope it helps," he says.

"Why wouldn't it?"

"It can take them a while to get used to new things."

"If they're really upset by the people and the cameras," I say, "I'll tell the soap company that the deal is off."

"Really?"

"Yes," I say, though things will have to get really bad before I say no. Orrin knows that and I know that because we need the money. We're having problems with the water heater in the trough. Even though it's early fall we've been having cool weather and it gets below freezing at night. I have to break the ice on the troughs in the morning. Unicorns won't drink if the water is too cold, and when they get dehydrated it can lead to colic and other intestinal problems. We need to replace the heater, and there's enough in the bank account to cover the cost, but that cuts down on the amount of money we'll have to buy hay and keep the blessing fed over the winter.

That afternoon when I check on the blessing grazing in the pasture, I make mental notes about which unicorns would be best for the soap commercial. I need unicorns with an even temperament, ones that will be calm around a bunch of new people and cameras. Those tend to be the roan and paint unicorns, not the white ones. I'm not sure why this is, but the classic white unicorns tend to have slightly larger horns and sharper tempers. I prefer the roans and paints anyway. They're prettier, in my opinion.

It's not always a good thing to promote the mysticism of unicorns. Some people buy unicorns for their horns, cut them off, grind them into a powder, and sell the rest as horsemeat. When I read news of an illegal horn-trading ring outside of Toronto last year, it made me shudder. I think the people I sell my unis to are good people, but how can I ever be sure?

WHEN ORRIN AND I make the ten-mile drive into town the next day to have lunch and buy groceries, everyone has heard the news of my soap commercial. The director called the only motel in town to make reservations for herself and the camera crew, and Bernice who works at the motel front desk had breakfast at the café this morning and told Myrna the waitress. Telling Myrna anything is like standing in the middle of town and shouting it over a megaphone.

Myrna and the other waitresses are already starstruck, asking if they can drive out to my ranch and bring their grandkids around when the camera crew is here.

"It would be educational for them," says Myrna. I figure she and the other waitresses hope to appear in the soap commercial. I say I don't know and I'll have to check with the director.

Orrin and I sit at the front counter like usual and order cheeseburgers. On Orrin's other side, Phil eats a grilled ham and cheese and grimaces at me.

"We don't need any Hollywood types coming out here," he says. "The only thing that will bring is more Hollywood types and then the town will go to shit."

"They're not from Hollywood," I say, "they're from St. Paul."

"Don't be an old stick-in-the-mud," says Myrna as she pours another cup of coffee for him. "You're just jealous that no one wants to film your cattle for a soap commercial."

"We need to keep our herds fed same as you do," Orrin says to Phil with a smile and a shrug. "You know what the times are like."

Phil mutters something I can't hear, but I don't imagine it's anything too bad because he likes Orrin. Most of the ranchers around here like Orrin more than they like me. He's not a transplant, and he sympathizes more with usual rancher concerns. I moved here from Ohio twenty years ago, but some people will always think of me as an outsider. I don't like the idea, but it is what it is.

Orrin and I spend the next two weeks figuring out which twenty unicorns from the sixty in the blessing would be good

105

candidates for the small screen. There's a lot to consider—which ones will be most photogenic and least camera-shy and most hospitable to strangers. I also have to sign a whole bunch of forms and waivers and other legal documents that the director sends in an inch-thick packet. Orrin and I drive to the café again, buy the town lawyer lunch, and get her to skim through everything and tell us what it means.

The lawyer orders a grilled cheese sandwich with mustard and home fries, and says that the forms state the film crew has insurance for their equipment and accidental injuries caused by my unicorns to the equipment or crew. I need to have insurance to cover injuries to my unicorns, and I have to keep reasonable control over them at all times.

"It's telling you that they have their rears covered, and making sure that you have your rear covered," she says.

"Why did they need a whole pile of papers to say that?" I ask. "Does it really take more than a page?"

She shrugs and sips her coffee. "We have to make sure those years of law school are worth something."

"You're going to be a huge TV star," says Myrna when she comes to refill my iced tea. "We can say we knew you when."

I say it's not me but my unicorns that will be in the spotlight. "I just want to keep them fed."

Myrna nods and smiles, but I know she sees me and the whole blessing of unicorns bound for Hollywood. Nobody seems to remember the crew is coming from St. Paul, which is colder and much less glamorous.

Phil sits at the counter two stools away from us.

"Blasted show animals," he mutters. "Not worth their oats."

In the past I got into debates with him and said that one of my unis could outwork a horse any day, but any battle with Phil is just wasted words.

Myrna keeps yapping about Orrin and me being bound for California. I get a little sick of it, and am almost happy when Phil breaks the conversation.

"Wolves got another two of my calves last night," he says loud enough to set everyone in the café grumbling.

"Pests," Orrin mutters. I glare at him but he just shrugs. "They don't belong here," he says.

"They were around here at the same time unicorns were," I say. "Not their fault the herds got shoved north to Canada."

"That doesn't mean we need to bring them back down," he says.

The scientists who've been reintroducing wolves to Wyoming say that disease kills more sheep and cattle than wolves, but when a wolf takes out a couple of sheep, everyone knows about it. It's not the same when a couple of sheep die of intestinal problems. Maybe I'm biased because unis can take care of themselves—they're territorial and they have that horn—so I don't worry about wolves taking out any members of the blessing.

Orrin's family is from the area, so he knows the difference between the way things used to be a generation or two ago and the way they are now. I've only been here for a couple of decades, so my definition of what is and is not normal is different. I feel bad for the wolves, but I'm the only rancher around who has any sympathy for them. The reality of nature is that humans moved the wolves out and the cattle in. Scientists are trying to restore the wild that was, but it has to coexist with fences and forage. That is not an easy feat.

THE DIRECTOR AND camera crew arrive at my ranch on a Monday morning, grumbling about the lack of good coffee shops in town. The café does a pretty good breakfast, but they're not experienced with making things to go. The director's frown gets even deeper when I explain my best candidates for the commercial are roan and paint unicorns. She wants white ones.

"They symbolize mysticism and purity and all that shit," she says. This is not her phone voice, this is her getting-down-to-business voice.

I take a deep breath.

"Oh," I say. After you've been around unicorns for a while and watched them take a dump, neither mysticism nor purity comes readily to mind. The people in the camera crew seem surprised when a big white unicorn shits in the pasture, which makes me smirk. What else are unicorns supposed to do? They eat hay, they make fertilizer. Simple as that.

"We can try using white ones," I say, "but they're going to be more temperamental. White ones don't always go where you want them to go."

The director paces.

"We need unicorn makeup," she says finally. "Paint on the horns. Powder to make the unicorns look more snowy and clean. That's what soap is all about."

Orrin and I drive into town and buy a lot of white talcum powder and shoe polish. We apply it to the unicorns in the pasture so they can watch us work, recognize each other more readily, and not be scared over their new, lighter coats.

"It's not bad," the director says finally. "We can fine-tune things later."

Then she's concerned my unicorns are not willowy enough.

"They look fat," she says.

I sigh. I spend a lot of time explaining the unicorn's build to prospective buyers. Unicorns are stockier than most people expect and have a heavier coat than horses, but they need that coat to survive in the wild. My unicorns are domesticated, but there are still some wild blessings in Canada. Willowy unicorns tend to have more colic and intestinal problems, so even selective breeding isn't a good idea unless you want a sick unicorn on your hands.

Members of the camera crew seem to like my unicorns more than the director, and ask if they can feed and pet them. Today they've come without their cameras and other equipment, since I think my unis should only have to deal with one confusing thing at a time.

I like the camera people—they're polite and easygoing and seem like they want to make friends with my unis. I spend two days with the camera crew and the unicorns in the pasture, giving them carrot and oat cookies to feed the unicorns, letting them scratch the unicorns behind their ears and around their horns, and teaching them the basics about unicorn body language. The most important thing is to pay attention to their ears. A unicorn's ears point in the direction of its interest, and that can shift pretty quickly. When a unicorn's head turns, the horn is sure to follow, and you have to watch for that. It's also important to notice when a uni's ears are flat against the sides of its head. That means an upset unicorn, and suggests you should get out of its way.

Working with five camera people and twenty unicorns is stressful because I have to pay attention to all twenty unis at once, and make sure no one looks scared or aggressive. The director doesn't spend as much time in the pasture as I'd like, she wants to be in town where she can get better cell phone reception and call people back in St. Paul to discuss other projects. I'm suspicious that she was turned off by the fact that my unicorns are not what she expected, but she still wants to shoot the commercial, so I guess it doesn't matter that much.

After their second day in the pasture, one of the guys from the camera crew asks me about buying a unicorn from me for his kids.

"Ever worked with large animals?" I say.

He says his grandfather had horses when he was growing up. "My kids keep asking for a pony," he says, "and there's a place where we could stable it outside of town."

I give him one of my brochures, tell him to think about buying a uni, and call me later. His interest makes me pleased and worried. It would be nice if the commercial would promote my ranch as well as soap, but there are always risks. Buying a unicorn is like buying a baby rabbit or duckling or Dalmatian puppy. It's a nice thought, but those pets are usually more work than the owner expected.

Unicorns are more finicky than horses, require more grain and less hay, and they're more susceptible to colic. They can also get horn rot if they're kept in a damp place for too long, so it's best to keep them in an open shelter rather than a stable. The white unis don't always like kids, but no matter how much I caution prospective buyers, some of them won't be dissuaded from buying a Diamond or Snowy or Cloud.

I've had more than one unicorn returned to me over the years because of ornery behavior. Snapping at kids. Refusing to be bridled. Stripping the bark off trees with their horns. I'll refund most of the money, but not the initial deposit. People get pissy about that, but it's a standard business practice.

In the evening after the camera crew has gone home, I hear a wolf howl and know a pack is near. It makes me smile, but Orrin grimaces.

"The unis will be fine," I say.

"That's not what I'm worried about," he says. "They don't belong here."

"They used to belong here."

"Not anymore."

"People could say the same thing about unis."

"They don't kill anything," he says.

I drop the subject because I know I'm not going to win.

THE NEXT DAY the camera crew arrives with their equipment and the director. They spend the morning setting up in one of my pastures, figuring out how they want to stage the shots and where they want the unicorns to run. Orrin and I herd ten unicorns into the round pen and let them sniff the camera and tripods. They're not scared of the equipment as much as they're curious about it, which makes me think the main problem won't be the unis running away from the cameras but getting too close.

In the afternoon we test out a few different camera angles. Orrin and I ride behind the blessing, driving them through the pasture like we do when we need to move the herd back to the round pen or barn or their winter shelter. We get three rounds of footage, everything goes well, and the director surveys my pastures to decide where she'd like to film next. Orrin and I stay mounted on our unicorns, but then I see Princess start.

I don't know what spooks her—it could be something small, an imagined movement in her peripheral vision—but it's enough to make her rear up and charge off, heading straight for the cluster of cameras and slamming into one that costs I don't want to know how much money. The camera person has enough time to get away, but I don't know if the camera is salvageable.

I yell and whistle to Princess. It takes a moment for her to calm down, but she walks to me slowly like a toddler who just threw a tantrum and knows she's in trouble. The director moans over the upset camera while I inspect Princess for wounds. There's a small cut above her leg, one I'll have Orrin tend to in a minute to make sure it doesn't get infected, but right now I have to tend to the director.

"What the fuck was that?" she says.

"She got upset by something," I say.

"I thought you had control over these animals," she says.

"I do," I say, "but I can't control everything they do. You can't control a dog or elephant or little kid all the time. I can be alert to their body language, but if something scares them..." I sigh. It's not the best of answers, but it's true.

"This camera is shot," she says.

"Don't you have insurance for that?"

"I'd hoped not to use it," she mutters. "And this limits the number of different angles we can shoot from at once." She glares at Princess. I roll my eyes. This is what happens when you use untrained animals.

The rest of the afternoon is wasted because the crew has to examine the camera and see if they can make repairs. They're calmer about the whole thing than the director, but they also like my unis more than she does.

The next day of shooting goes better. The director arrives with a larger cup of coffee. Extra caffeine may improve her mood. We shoot in two different sections of the pasture, get footage of my unis running over a hill and past the little wooded section of my property, then we get another angle of them running diagonally toward and past the camera crew. Life is good, the unis are well-behaved in all their false white glory, and the director almost smiles.

"This isn't that bad," I tell Orrin that evening as we feed the blessing and give them the daily once-over, looking for runny eyes or flesh wounds.

"Sure," he says, glancing out to the pasture.

"What's wrong?"

"My mind is still on that wolf."

"They won't hurt the unis."

"It's not the unis," he says, "it's everything else. It's not good for anyone in the area."

"They don't take that many sheep."

"Two is more than enough," he says. "You'd feel different if it was your profit being gobbled up."

I bite my lip because I can't disagree.

THE DIRECTOR AND camera crew arrive early the next morning, before sunrise, because she wants to get a shot of the herd galloping through the pasture as the sun paints the sky Wyoming pink. Orrin and I ride out with them but I notice the blessing is restless and edgy. Something is not right. They always see changes before I do.

Over a hill near my property line, I see what they smelled.

Beside the barbed wire fence, a wolf lies dead. Gored.

"Oh my God," says the director.

The camera people gasp.

"They protect themselves all right," says Orrin.

I dismount and walk to the wolf. It hasn't been dead for long. We'll have to bury it before it gets much warmer. Five minutes after we discover the wolf, a group of eight unicorns pads over the hill. Corduroy, one of my pure white stallions, has blood on his horn and forehead.

It doesn't surprise me. Corduroy is one of the bolder males, a self-appointed alpha guard of the blessing. The camera crew gasps again. The blood against his white horn and forehead is stark, but the reality of the horn is that it's not just for show.

112

I scratch Corduroy behind the ear, a place where it's not bloody, because he was doing what he's supposed to do, protect the herd.

I think a few members of the camera crew are ready to throw up, but when you work with animals you get used to blood and shit and everything else. If you don't have a sturdy stomach, ranching is not for you.

"I think we should go back to the motel for the rest of the morning," the director says. "You need to deal with...what needs to be dealt with."

I agree that would be best.

Orrin and I dig a hole on the edge of the property line while the unicorns graze around us. They aren't nervous so I don't think the rest of the wolves are nearby. Orrin and I wear leather work gloves when we move the wolf to the hole, but I can feel the softness of its fur through the leather. I don't cry, but I'm upset. This must have happened two centuries ago when wolves and unicorns were both roaming these plains, but it's sad to see something beautiful die.

After we bury the wolf, I lead Corduroy to the barn so I can wash off his horn and forehead. The blood is dry so it takes more than a little scrubbing to get the stain off, and I can't get the earthy tinge out of his coat. That will have to be cleaned by the rain over the next few weeks. Corduroy is oddly patient while I tend to his horn and coat. I'm sure he wants to rid himself of the smell of blood as much as I want to see him clean again.

The camera people return around two in the afternoon. We get two more hours of footage, including filming the unis at sunset (to replace the shot we missed at sunrise). The members of the camera crew are more edgy than before, start when a unicorn whinnies or stomps or shakes its head suddenly. Their nervousness transfers to my unicorns, and it's harder to make them behave.

"We have enough footage," the director tells me at dusk.

"I thought you were going to stay one more day," I say.

"We have enough," she says again. "This won't decrease your paycheck, if that's what you're worried about."

"No," I say. I don't want them to leave with a negative impression. Any large animal can be dangerous if you're not careful, the trick is not to be scared and to pay attention to their body language. The guy who wanted to buy a unicorn is staying further away from them than before, and I figure he won't call me about a purchase in the near future. I'm a little sad and a little relieved.

With the camera crew out of our lives, I figure everything will get back to normal. This is true until two in the afternoon the following day, when Orrin and I drive into town and discover my unis have become wolf-slaying heroes. Even Phil is grudgingly pleased.

"Those show animals finally provided a service," he says.

It makes me mad, even if I can admit this was the way of things when there were no ranchers with barbed wire fences and we didn't force animals to obey property lines. I don't always like the dirt and blood and inherent messiness of life on the plains, how nature is so often less than tidy, but that's what I get for wanting to live closer to the land than most people. At least now my unicorns can go back to being themselves, without powder and shoe polish, and they'll have grain to eat through the winter.

Four months later, when my unis finally make it to the small standardized screen, I've almost forgotten about the commercial except for the fact that I don't have to panic every time I see a bank statement in the mail. I'm not the first person in town to watch it. Myrna is, since she's always got the TV on at the café. When Orrin and I stop in for cheeseburgers, she makes us sit down at the front counter and refills our coffee cups until the commercial appears. This process consumes forty minutes of channel-flipping, during which Myrna will not let me go to the bathroom.

"What if you miss it?" she says, gripping my wrist with one hand and the remote with the other.

I resist the urge to say, "What if I wet my pants because you won't let me go to the ladies' room?" Myrna doesn't have time for such logic.

"There!" she says, sighing and letting go of my wrist when a purple screen flashes on TV after a toothpaste commercial. The advertisement starts with a shot of my unis running across the field at sunset. A giant bar of soap rises behind them like a huge moon and hovers over the field like a big pale spaceship, while an announcer says something about feeling mystically clean and pure. There's a second shot of my unicorns, without the soap backdrop, charging in another direction. The commercial has more unicorns than soap, but I guess that's how people sell things now.

"Not bad," I say, rubbing my wrist.

Orrin rolls his eyes. "I have to pee," he says.

Myrna clasps her hands together and sighs. "Well, I think it was just lovely," she says.

I thank Myrna for the coffee and excuse myself to use the bathroom.

Over the next week Orrin and I become minor celebrities in town, or at least people stop me in the bank and grocery and café and tell me they saw the unis on TV. Some people say the unis look great. Other people say they saw the unis and leave it at that.

When Orrin and I see Phil at the café, he just harrumphs.

"I suppose your wolf-killers are okay if they know their place," he says.

Town is not flooded with director types wearing sunglasses and leather jackets, or picture-snapping paparazzi driving around in SUVs, but that's one of the benefits of living in the middle of nowhere. Myrna doesn't let the lack of stardom sway her devotion. No matter what she's doing, she stops to watch the commercial when it comes on TV at the café. If she's tallying a receipt at the register, she quits punching numbers. If she's slicing a pie, she pauses with the knife in the air. If she's refilling cups of coffee, she sets down the pot and picks it up again when my unis disappear from the screen. Many customers roll their eyes, but Myrna doesn't notice because she's too busy yapping about how my unis are famous.

"All across America, people are watching those unicorns," she says. "Our unicorns." Myrna has decided my unicorns belong to the town, at least in some spiritual sense. Other people have started to appreciate my unis as well, for a variety of reasons.

Since the wolf incident, three sheep ranchers purchased two unis each to protect their herds. One of the ranchers told me the unis will pay for themselves in the number of lambs they'll save. I don't want to stop the ranchers from buying unicorns, these are my best sales all year, but I don't like the reason for their purchases.

Orrin says, "We're selling unicorns. That's a good thing."

"I'm not raising my unis to be prized for killing things," I say.

"You're too picky," he says. "Those sheep ranchers will take good care of the unis."

"I know," I say. But frankly I'd rather they do more commercials.

Because we can't have the entire blessing crowd into our front yard to watch TV and sharpen their horns on the side of the house, most of my unicorns will never see their thirty seconds of fame. But I do bring Lavender inside the fence, because I want at least one unicorn to see the final product. She's a calm and thoughtful mare, and strikes me as the unicorn most likely to appreciate cinema.

"This is crazy," Orrin tells me, but he rolls the TV over to the window anyway. I hold Lavender's bridle as she watches the commercial, peering at herself and the other unis and occasionally flicking her ear. When the commercial is over, she noses me for a carrot and oat cookie since she knows I have one in my pocket.

"So what did you think?" I say, giving her the cookie. Lavender crunches on her treat, unwilling to give me feedback, but perhaps she's wondering about those lovely white creatures galloping into the sunset, and why those hills looked so much like home.

Sisyphus

HE WAS AN old man, so no one understood his muscles. In the grocery store where he worked as a bagger, he helped elderly ladies carry sacks of food to their cars, hefting five on each arm. Everyone stared, but the old man couldn't pick up an egg without an intense and concentrated effort to be gentle, otherwise he crushed the shells. He'd spent too long rolling that damned stone up the hill. The old man could only work hard and fast, that's what he'd done for centuries, so when he opened his apartment door the first time he put the knob through the opposite wall and left a nasty hole. He had to pretend the world was made of glass threads.

Every day the old man went to the senior center to take watercolor painting classes and buy a cheap cafeteria lunch. He worked two jobs, as a bag boy and gas station cashier. Everyone at the senior center sympathized. They were on limited budgets, and lunchtime conversation consisted of how much they were spending on food, rent, and medications. Prices were always going up.

BECAUSE SHE'D BEEN an elementary school secretary and was therefore a compassionate person, Helen, one of his friends from the senior center, offered to take the old man out for dinner.

"My treat," she said.

The old man shook his head. "You're too kind," he said, but Helen was waiting to pick him up at his apartment when he arrived home the next evening. She was as determined as he was strong, and she'd been lonely since her husband died. Helen liked the idea of dating a man who enjoyed watercolor painting and could lift two hundred pounds with one hand.

As they ate cheeseburgers and fries and drank chocolate milkshakes, she told him about spending thirty-five years as a secretary. He told her about spending several decades as a Greek king, which surprised Helen since at first glance he didn't seem the kingly sort. When she squinted, however, she could tell that behind his wrinkles he'd once been a very attractive man.

"But not a very good king," he said. "I bet you were a much better secretary."

"Not at all," said Helen, who believed in thinking the best of everyone. "I'm sure you were a wonderful king. You're so helpful cleaning up after our painting class."

She wasn't prepared for him to take another sip of milkshake and unroll a teary story about ordering his soldiers to kill people who he thought might question his right to be in power.

Helen bit her lip. "But you know that was wrong now, don't you, honey?"

The old man nodded, sniffled, and resumed drinking his milkshake.

Helen had never met royalty before, but she took it in stride because she figured those kinds of people were like everyone else, they'd just been born in the right place at the right time to the right people. She'd been born into a life that led her to be a school secretary, which meant three and a half decades of juggling phone calls, lunches left at home, copy machine repairs, and sending some "sick" kids to the school nurse and some back to class though they protested that they were feeling "icky." A hectic but fulfilling career. If someone had given her a chance to rewrite sections of her life, Helen only would have taken up watercolor painting a bit sooner.

AT THE SENIOR center, the old man yawned when he stayed late after the watercolor painting class.

"You look exhausted," Helen said, touching his shoulder.

"I'm fine," said the old man, straightening his posture, but the two jobs wore on him so he was grateful when Helen dragged him out to dinner again. She wanted more of his story, and asked how he'd fallen from kingship. The old man was grudging but obliged because she'd paid for his cheeseburger and seemed genuinely concerned. No living person knew the full tale, and he admitted that confessional therapy was a bit of a relief.

"When I died the first time," the old man said, "I told my wife not to bury my body but lay it out with no ceremony. Hades was upset that she didn't follow the proper rites, so he sent me back to the land of the living. I reigned as king for another thirty years until I died again."

"How resourceful," said Helen. "You bought yourself three extra decades."

The old man sighed. "Yes, but Hades was so angry that when I died a second time, I had to roll a boulder up a hill every day. It rolled back down at sunset and I repeated the process. After a few centuries it wasn't a strain, but I pretended it was difficult. Then I let my guard down and started pushing the boulder with one hand, showing off a little, so Hades devised a new torture."

Helen frowned. "He didn't hurt you, did he? Brand you with hot irons? Run you through with a sword?"

"He returned me to the land of the living and condemned me to work in gas stations and grocery stores," said the old man. "Hades knew nothing would be worse for a former ruler than an eternity of minimum-wage labor."

The old man shuddered. He'd wanted to escape death and reign as a king, not dwell among the masses who could barely make rent. Decoding the cash register had been the most difficult task. It was like a stone with buttons that beeped annoyingly for weeks until he learned the right numerical patterns to punch. His chariot had been replaced by a rattling secondhand Lincoln

Town Car. His feasts of mutton were reduced to ramen noodles and senior center lunches that were too high in sodium. His days were plagued by customers who yelled at him when he couldn't make change fast enough. They didn't know he was a king, not a commoner. Even worse, if they had known, they wouldn't have cared.

In the evening he came home smelling like grease and cigarettes, wishing for his old routine of boulder and hill. He didn't realize how much he'd come to relish that regularity. If he returned to the underworld, Hades had promised to hang poisonous snakes from every inch of his body. The poison wouldn't kill him since he was already dead, but it would hurt like anything.

HELEN'S FRIENDS WORRIED over her because she'd mentioned that the old man's past was a little shady. They repeated tales they'd heard on the nightly news, stories of women who'd fallen in love with convicts, men who were all sweetness and light until they got their claws into a lady's skin. Helen shook her head and said not to worry, but she was concerned when, over another dinner of burgers and fries, the old man told her about his past business ventures.

"I tried selling get-out-of-hell insurance," he said.

"You can get people out of hell?" Helen said.

"The underworld, really," he said, "but hell sounded better. It isn't a fun place for most shades. Terribly boring, and the coffee is awful."

Helen nodded, though this wasn't the image of hell she tended to conjure.

"I went door to door wearing a white shirt and tie and dark pants," he said. "Most of the population is worried about the end of the world, and I've always been good at capitalizing on those kinds of opportunities. But I didn't realize you needed a vendor's license to sell things. The authorities weren't happy. I didn't realize how much times had changed."

Helen allowed that was true. Her health-nut daughter called three times a week to tell Helen about the results of the latest scientific study, which new drug or herb or chemical you were supposed to take or not take. Helen's daughter wanted to manage the well-being of the world, but she settled for her family's and Helen's.

"Dear, I think you're overreacting," Helen said every time.

"I'm not overreacting," said her daughter. "Potato chips could kill us. The kids are never eating them ever again, and you shouldn't, either."

Helen sighed. Her daughter was a victim of the computer age and accompanying information overload. Helen had yet to master e-mail, and her life was no worse for it.

"We didn't know about all these dangers when I was growing up and we're still alive," she told her daughter.

"The earth was more pure when you were growing up," said her daughter. "There weren't all these damn chemicals. I'm coming over tomorrow with a new water purification system for your apartment."

It was easier for Helen to allow her daughter to do whatever she wanted, since that was the best way to calm her down before the next scientific study was released. Helen didn't tell her daughter about her real aches and pains, but she was almost as frustrated with her body as she was with her daughter. It had always been so placid and cooperative before, yet now she felt like everything was being replaced, piece by slow piece, with the body of an old person. Seventy-three was not old. Not when you were seventy-three. Her body had other things to say, however. Parts were wearing out, wearing down, wearing thin, though her mind felt the same as ever. Helen was thoroughly indignant when her daughter said she was forgetful and should take a seaweed extract. Sometimes there were a couple of misplaced facts in Helen's head, but since she had more facts to catalog than younger people, occasionally information was shelved in some out-of-the-way bookcase in a corner. That didn't mean she was *old*.

HELEN WAS STRICKEN when she went to lunch at the senior center and discovered that Vivian had died. It was sudden, a late-night stroke at home, nothing the doctors could have done. Helen plodded to the visitation and funeral and listened morosely while her friends mused that Vivian looked downright chipper in the casket. But later, at the memorial luncheon, everyone was antsy. Young as they felt, most knew they could count their remaining years on their fingers and toes.

"We should try to get her back," the old man said as he and Helen left the luncheon.

"Back from where?" asked Helen, though she knew what he meant and was excited and terrified by the idea.

"I want to see if I can do it," he said. "I have connections."

"But the snakes Hades threatened you with...," said Helen with a shudder.

"Yes, the snakes," said the old man and paused. "After working a double shift yesterday, the snakes seem less imposing. I'm willing to take the risk."

Helen nodded. "That's very kind, but Vivian...well, I don't know if she'd come with you." Viv hadn't exactly trusted the old man. She was the one who said he'd go through Helen's purse and steal her credit cards.

The old man knitted his eyebrows. "Would you consider coming with me?"

"Would I make it back?" Helen asked. She figured that Hades wouldn't look kindly on the living venturing into the land of the dead.

"Well, probably," said the old man.

Helen bit her lower lip. She had *something* left to lose, her earthly existence, but she'd always been a woman who was too curious for her own good.

The old man explained that the entrance to the underworld wasn't exactly a place. There was no door or crack in some mountain, spirits simply appeared at the underworld's entrance once they left their bodies. As they stood in her living room, the old man took Helen's hand in his surprisingly warm fingers, then told Helen to close her eyes since the transition was rather bright. She saw the flash through her eyelids, illuminating blood vessels. When Helen opened her eyes again they were standing on a moving walkway. It looked like a long airport corridor, drab and metallic with buzzing lights overhead.

Clustered around them were people wearing gray. The new shades. Some read newspapers. Some filed their nails. The sidewalk moved at an unbearably slow pace, so the old man excused himself and Helen as they wove past shades who didn't glance up. At the end of the walkway the old man nodded to a younger one wearing dark glasses and a blue uniform. He nodded back. They walked through the turnstile door beside the young man, and entered the land of the dead.

It was a wide flat field populated by more people in gray. The grass was tinged blue and the sky was gray-green like it was before a summer storm in the Midwest. The temperature wasn't bad, not too hot or cold, but a little…unsettling. Helen and the old man walked past card tables, shades playing chess and checkers and drinking from white Styrofoam cups.

"They have a choice of water or watery coffee, but the flavor isn't worth it," said the old man. "The first thing I did when I left was order a triple shot of espresso. *That* was heaven."

The shades didn't look cheery or depressed. Just bored.

Helen and the old man wandered over a few hills, scanning flat gray faces until they found Vivian playing solitaire beside a tree. She wore a shapeless charcoal-colored sweater and skirt, but jumped up when she saw her visitors and ran over to Helen. Viv didn't look much different than when she'd been alive. She'd favored drab tones but had a bright and generally opinionated personality to make up for it.

"We found you," said Helen.

"You came to be with me," said Vivian, embracing her.

Helen shook her head. "Come back with us. Everyone misses you."

Vivian frowned. "You're not dead? The living aren't supposed to be here. And what's he doing with you?" She nodded at the old man standing behind Helen.

"I have connections—" the old man began.

"I don't want to go back," said Vivian. "Why don't you stay here?"

Helen swallowed hard. "I came to get you," she said in a whisper-thin voice, wondering what had become of her volume. Perhaps it had been swallowed in the gray air. "It wasn't your time to go yet."

"Why not?" said Vivian, crossing her arms. Helen hadn't expected that.

"Your granddaughter is getting married in the spring, and your grandsons are graduating, and your youngest is pregnant and you said you'd help her with housework because her legs have swelled something awful," Helen said, rattling off the list of things Vivian often spoke about at lunch. "I thought she was going on bed rest. If you're not there I don't know what her husband will do with the three-year-old and six-year-old and—"

"Get a decent sitter and quit relying on me," Vivian said, sitting back down. "I haven't had a break like this in years."

Helen shook her head. Vivian had been four years younger than her, and she knew Viv's daughter needed help.

"Come now," said Vivian gently. "Have a blueberry muffin. They're very good, and I know you love blueberries."

She opened her palm and a muffin appeared, sweet and golden with a streusel topping. Helen was hungry and reached out to take the muffin, but the old man grabbed her elbow.

"Lovely visiting," he said, "but we really must go. Have a wonderful respite from all your earthly concerns."

Vivian frowned. "I thought Helen wanted the muffin."

"I do want the muffin," said Helen.

"No, you don't," said the old man. "We had lunch an hour ago. Think of your figure."

Helen blushed. "We just got here. Can't we stay and chat for a moment?"

"No," hissed the old man, "we can't."

"Bye, Vivian dear," Helen yelled as the old man dragged her away. "Have a lovely, um, afterlife!"

Vivian harrumphed, returned to her card game, and stuffed half the muffin in her mouth.

"It looked like a good muffin." Helen tried to tug her hand from the old man's grasp.

"Not good enough to stay here forever," he muttered. A door appeared in the field in front of them, one that looked very much like Helen's bathroom door. He opened it and they were back in her apartment. Helen crossed her arms.

"We could have played one game of cards," she said.

"Do you know what your friend was trying to do?" said the old man.

Helen shook her head. "She was being cordial. Viv made the best muffins."

"If you'd eaten the food of the dead, you would have had to remain in the underworld."

Helen gaped, then slowly closed her mouth. "Not Vivian," she murmured. "She'd never do something like that."

"The dead get lonely," said the old man. "I'm sorry. We shouldn't have risked going there. The shades are a greater danger to you than Hades."

"It was my choice to visit and I'm glad I did," said Helen, but goose bumps covered her arms and legs. Death could change people, and not always for the better.

"I suppose I shouldn't bother you anymore at the senior center," said the old man.

"Not at all," said Helen. If the trip had taught her anything, it was that this particular old man did indeed have connections. He wasn't someone she wanted out of her life yet.

As they had their usual burgers and fries for dinner, her mind blossomed with the possibilities. She could go see friends. Her late husband. Her parents. Her great-grandparents, including the great-great-grandmother who had supposedly sailed from Germany with gold coins sewn into her dress. There were too many stories she wanted to have explained and verified, danger be hanged.

Helen patted the old man's hand across the table and he smiled back at her. He might not have grinned if he'd known the thoughts whirring in her head, but she wasn't going to tell him yet. Those plans could unroll slowly as she dreamed just how many biographies she'd write, and the family tree roots she'd dig up now that she had the time and the source material.

She'd always thought of death as an awful unknown weight, but it wasn't nearly so monstrous now that she understood the mystery. Death was merely a game of comings and goings, like an extended vacation to a rather drab resort. It would take some convincing, but the old man seemed to believe in risks and adrenaline rushes. He was bored with his jobs and thus easily tempted by the thrill of covert operations.

Helen rested her fingers on the back of the old man's hand and gave him a peculiar smile. He would come to know it was the one she used when she was plotting something new.

Feet

BECAUSE HE'S SIXTY-FIVE years old, weighs five hundred pounds, and is mostly retired, my father is learning how to levitate. He claims he's managed to float a few inches off the couch when he concentrates hard, but that only happens when I'm at work in the shoe store. I've seen him make our salt and pepper shakers rise two inches off the kitchen table, a pretty neat trick, but they only weigh a few ounces, not five hundred pounds. Still, Dad is not one to be daunted when he wants something. '

"Walking is annoying," Dad says as he takes another waffle out of the iron and slathers it with two tablespoons of butter. Dad waddles to the table and sits across from me, douses the waffle with syrup, and cuts it into neat pieces with the side of his fork. For such a big guy, Dad eats very delicately. He spends most of his time on our couch, doesn't sleep on his bed because if he lay down he'd suffocate under his weight.

"Would you leave the apartment if you could float?" I say. Before Dad became an invalid he got stares huffing down the street. A floating fat guy would be even more of an attraction.

"I don't know if I could get out the door," says Dad. "It's gotten smaller since we moved in. We need someone to widen it."

But Dad doesn't want a bigger door, he wants newspaper headlines when people try to extract him from our living room. It's his contingency plan if floating doesn't work.

"All I need before I die is the fifteen minutes of fame Andy Warhol promised to everyone," he says.

I kiss my dad on the top of his gray head and head to work on foot. I don't mind walking though I'm not tiny—five foot eight and one hundred eighty pounds. Dad says it makes me look substantial. Mom says it's genetic. She's the same size as me and lives in Georgia, works for a modeling agency that specializes in plus-sized women. She says I should quit the shoe business and work for her, but I love the store too much to abandon it.

Besides, who'd look after my fretting floating father?

I unlock the front door at 9:30 and run a sweeper over the carpet before Scott, my one employee, arrives at 9:45. He's forty-one, has a middle-aged-guy paunch, glasses, dark hair, and what Dad likes to call "a believable smile." Scott makes sure the windows and counter are clean, there are full bowls of lavender potpourri in every corner, and a Hayden CD on the speakers. I try to set the mood for buying shoes.

Ten years ago, when Dad was still managing the shop, he decided to specialize in orthopedics for people with foot problems. Our foot-friendly sandals and pumps are hot items with ladies, but elderly gentlemen come in wanting dressy shoes that don't pinch. I love seeing customers smile when they realize how much better their entire body feels once they have the right shoes.

Many of my older customers say their feet are changing— getting arthritic, growing callouses and corns and bunions. Some of them have gout so their toe joints swell to the size of golf balls. Others develop plantar fasciitis so it feels like their heels are on fire. Some say their feet have turned into bricks. I've learned that aging is all about negotiating with your body, making allowances to deal with its shifting form and abilities.

My customers are glad I understand that.

I have sweet ones like Mrs. Tiller, who loves sequined pumps and brings oatmeal cookies, cranky ones like Mr. Dubler, who gets dragged in by his wife for penny loafers, and needy ones like Mrs. Germaine, who expects me to follow at her elbow the whole time she's in the store.

At six in the evening, an hour before we close, an elderly lady waddles into the store and demands I take back a pair of athletic shoes and give her a full refund. She wears jeans, a purple blouse, silver heart earrings, and a sour expression.

"You said the shoes would feel good, but my feet still hurt," the lady says.

I examine her sales receipt and the shoes. They have scuff marks on the soles and sides.

"Ma'am," I say, "you've had these shoes for a month."

"Yes," says the lady, "and my feet still hurt."

She takes off her socks and shoes to show me neat rows of silver tacks piercing her feet. I wince because I often have customers with tiny glass beads on their toes, bumps you can't scrape off, though I haven't seen anything like these tacks in a couple of years. That was when a lady came in with an awful case of chilblains. She had screws stuck in her feet, at least eight rows of them, but that was a matter of finding shoes to keep her feet warm and dry in cool weather.

"The doctors can't do anything about tacks," says the lady, sliding her socks back on.

This is when my job gets tricky. Even the best shoes can't alleviate all pain, and I won't take her purchase back if she's worn them for weeks.

"You need different support insoles," I say. "I'll give you some for free."

"You said my feet wouldn't hurt if I bought these shoes," says the lady.

"They didn't hurt for a month," I say. "We need to renegotiate, see what kind of support they need."

"If I knew you were going to be impolite," she says, "I wouldn't have come to this store."

"I'll get your insoles," I say, turning around so she can't see me grimace.

Sometimes the customer is not always right. Sometimes the customer is a bit of a pain, though if I had tacks in my feet I'd be ill-tempered. It's hard to explain the constraints of medicine and footwear, how doctors and shoe salespeople can only work certain kinds of magic though we wish we could do more. When I give the lady her insoles, she glares at me like I handed her a fungus and stomps out of the store. I glance at Scott. He shrugs.

It's one of those nights when I'm too happy to change the open sign to closed.

Dad makes chicken parmesan for dinner. I keep quiet while he eats enough for four people. I'm his daughter, not his mother, and lectures make his eyes and ears turn to steel. When Dad says he floated six inches off the floor today, I congratulate him and don't mention the irked lady. I took over his store eight years ago, when I was twenty-seven, and I want to solve problems on my own, even when the customers or their feet are unruly.

After dinner Dad tries to demonstrate his levitation skills while sitting on the couch. He grits his teeth like he's constipated, but mutters it takes that kind of resolve to escape gravity and the constraints of his body.

"There we go," he grunts. "I'm floating about a inch above the cushions."

But he's so heavy and the couch is so squishy that I can't tell if he's lifting up or if his feet pressed against the floor are doing the work.

"Nice," I say, trying not to sound like a mother praising her four-year-old's drawings.

"You don't believe me," mutters Dad.

"It's subtle," I say.

"I made chocolate cake for dessert," he says. "Be a sweetie and cut us both a piece."

After cake, Dad practices floating condiment jars across the kitchen table. He moves the mustard and the dill pickles and even the economy-size ketchup bottle, but that makes him break a sweat. I hope working magic burns a few calories in mental effort.

MELVIN HAS BEEN coming to the store for years, gets awful gout and his toe joints swell to the size of marshmallows. He used to visit with his wife, Henriette, but she had a stroke last year and passed away. Today Melvin says his toes are made of lead and he can't bend them. He takes off one sock and shoe to show me the gray metal of his foot. I wonder if it's more of a circulation than a support problem, but I say I'll see what I can do.

"You're a sweetheart," says Melvin, who's as kind and considerate a customer as I could want. But sweet must be countered with sour, so I'm not surprised when the whiny lady from yesterday walks into the store, plops down on a chair, and crosses her arms. She wears a long denim skirt, dark pink blouse, and the same sour expression.

"I want my money back," she says.

"The insoles are the best we can do," I say. "Did you try them?"

"I want my money back," she repeats.

I say, "I'd like to work with your feet. We can figure this out together."

She shakes her head and crosses her arms more tightly. She still has those tacks piercing her toes and only a refund will do.

I let her sit. And sit. And sit. I can be sympathetic, but I'm also as stubborn as anyone else, and there are some store policies I can't break. The lady pouts in silence for ten minutes, then starts talking to Melvin.

"The shoes here are bad quality," she says, following him around the store. "She won't take them back."

Melvin examines boots while my face turns a slow red. I want to do more than I can, but my powers of negotiation with feet are limited. Most customers appreciate that fact, but when they can't understand it, I get mad. I don't want to give her a lecture on helplessness, how I've seen feet with steel nails through them, feet that were in so much pain it made me want to cry, so I march over and say I've done what I can.

"I'm willing to work with you," I say, "but if you bother patrons, I'll call the police."

"Go ahead," she says. "They need to hear about this injustice."

The lady sits down and smirks. I walk to the front register and the phone, but hear her say "Lord, not again."

She holds out her legs straight out. Her feet have disappeared, and her face crinkles like she might cry. Melvin wrinkles his nose, pads over, and pats the footless woman on the shoulder.

"My feet disappeared last week," he says. "I couldn't leave the house for a day."

"It happened to me around this time last year." The lady shakes her head. "I went to the doctor but she couldn't do much but prescribe another drug to alleviate the symptoms so I could hobble around with a walker. I don't want a walker or more drugs."

"Too many medications," sighs Melvin.

The old lady nods and looks at her feet.

"Should I call a cab?" I ask from the register, but neither of the old people hears me. I wait on another customer who wants a pair of patent leather Mary Janes. When I glance back to the old lady, her feet have reappeared and she's testing her balance on the arm of the chair. I watch her hesitant hobble, feel bad but hope she won't return.

In the break room I take a few tacks out of the bulletin board, remove my socks and my shoes, and test them on the bottoms of my feet. I wince at the piercing pressure, can't make myself push in the point enough to draw blood. When I think about that lady, my feet ache. I want to grab her shoulders and scream my frustration. I am not a miracle worker, but medicine and footwear have gotten so advanced that people expect their pains to melt away, like every doctor is Merlin with a stethoscope and I'm a shoe store fairy who turns bunions into blossoms.

DAD MAKES spaghetti and meatballs for dinner and looks depressed. He says he couldn't levitate anything today, not even the tooth-pick holder. It feels like he's regressing.

"I thought I'd found the key to escaping the ground," he says, "but it keeps slipping away. All I want is to be a balloon."

I imagine Dad floating out the window. We could tether him to the roof of the apartment, so he could shout down the wind speed and temperature and air pressure. I twirl pasta around my fork and resist the urge to tell Dad he shouldn't have a fifth help-ing.

Quarter after two in the morning and I sit up in bed, gasp-ing. I think I had a bad dream, but then I hear Dad wheeze in the living room. I scurry into the hall and find he's rolled off the couch and is squatting on the floor. His body is bigger and wider and flatter, plush and navy blue. His arms have rounded, and he holds them parallel to the floor. His feet have shrunk to the size of pool balls, and his knees have morphed into two cushions.

My father has become a loveseat. One we wouldn't be able to get out the door.

I imagine the headline: "Man launches second career as living room furniture."

Dad gasps once more, then stops breathing.

I scurry for the phone, but hear his whisper: "No, don't."

In a few moments he's back to being Dad, sitting on the couch and breathing heavily.

I ease next to him. "How do you feel?"

"Fine," he says.

"You should go to the doctor to see if anything is wrong," I say. "Your breathing—"

"No," says Dad. "When it's my time, it's my time. Be a dear and get your dad a piece of that chocolate cake."

Usually I'd obey, but now I shake my head and go back to my bedroom.

"Float there yourself," I mutter.

WHEN THE OLD lady marches into the store just after two in the afternoon, I'm with Melvin looking at penny loafers. He gets a new pair every year, and is very serious about choosing the right style. I note the lady's feet are back to normal, chat with Melvin as she strides to the display of athletic shoes. She picks up a box, turns around, and walks to the exit. When she's ten feet away, I sprint for the door, grab the old lady's arm, and shove her in a chair next to the register. I'm not gentle with shoplifters.

"Ow," she yelps.

I say, "What the hell were you doing?"

"Getting a replacement pair of shoes," she says. "This process has taken too long."

"You were stealing," I say.

"The first shoes weren't any good," she says.

"We'll explain that to the police," I say.

Her wail is so loud it shakes the entire store. Scott and Melvin and I stare. The lady starts crying, releasing so many tears she soaks her jeans and dampens the carpet. I want to cry, too. I'm supposed to solve problems for my customers, not want to shoot them. It's desperation and sympathy and annoyance that make me sit next to her and bawl. I'm tired. Of her. Of my father. Of all the feet I want to save. If you don't get that emotion out of your system you'll explode, and that's messier than damp carpets.

When we're both dry-eyed and sitting in puddles, Scott walks to the bathroom for paper towels to mop everything up. Melvin says, "After my wife died I had to sit in the bathtub for four days after the funeral so I wouldn't flood the house."

Scott hands me a wad of tissues. All my makeup washed off but I feel better, go to the bathroom to finish drying off. When I come out, Melvin and the woman are gone. I hope they went to get pizza and talk about ways to negotiate with their bodies, find truces and other spots of temporary agreement.

Maybe when I get back to the apartment my dad will have had a similar conference with his body. But on my walk home I know I have to steel myself for the day when he'll free himself of the constraints of logic and gravity, move out and up like the balloon he wants to be.

Sphinx

I KEPT THE sphinx in my front yard. I'd wanted one for a long time, the way other people want a Dalmatian or Persian cat. It wasn't just because the houses on my block all looked the same, small and marked only with the occasional tulip bed or stray tricycle, though that was part of it. The sphinx was mostly for safety reasons. I'd always been a nervous person and the nightly news was thick with burglary reports. Some robber, maybe even a gang, was swiping TVs and computers and DVD players and raiding jewelry boxes. I spent the money my boyfriend thought I was saving for a new car to buy the sphinx and have it shipped from Egypt. The moment it stepped out of that wooden crate and sniffed the humid July air, I was in love.

It was a regular guard sphinx, five feet at the shoulder with a lion's body and human head, not one of the deluxe models with eagle wings. I'd wanted something larger, but it would have been more difficult to transport, and this sphinx was still a good foot taller than me when I took its head into account.

From the start my boyfriend did not like the sphinx, wondered why I'd bought it.

"It's too big to cuddle with," he said. "Too big to fit in the house." He never was an animal lover. I reminded him it was the smallest sphinx available, the most economical model, but this did not sway him.

"I don't like the way it looks at me sideways," he said, crossing his arms as we stood in the front yard.

"It's getting used to you," I said as the sphinx bent to lick its paw.

"I wouldn't want to be alone with it," he said, walking into the house.

My boyfriend and I had been arguing a lot lately, snipping at each other and not kissing much. When we'd started going out he didn't mind eating at home and watching movies after dinner, but now he said we needed to go out more. He tried to convince me to get drinks with him and his friends, but after a day at the insurance office I was tired of talking. I needed to rest.

"I get bored," he said. "You need to live a little."

"I want to relax," I said. "Not be around people."

"I don't understand why working eight hours in an office can make you so exhausted," he muttered. I tried to explain how it wasn't just work, it was hearing about loss all day, it was trying to comfort weeping people over the phone when they got their payment from the insurance company and it wasn't enough.

"Just leave work at work," he said.

Easy enough for him since he was a bank teller.

I pretended to sleep. He said his friends thought I was anti-social.

On the weekends he stayed out even longer, sometimes until two in the morning. I watched the local news before bed and was reminded of the latest break-ins. I hated being alone, wanted the comfort of another person, and sometimes he forgot to lock the door at night. After buying the sphinx I felt better.

The sphinx responded to basic commands. Sit. Lie down. Come here. Fetch. It couldn't speak, though. I wasn't sure how it managed to purr. The sphinx liked romping in the front yard, which made sense because it had spent a few millennia completely stationary on a pedestal. I'm sure it was tired of heat and pyramids laden with jewels and gold and dead pharaohs. Now it only had to protect my TV and furniture and laptop—not as exciting, but maybe lower stress. The sphinx could not smell, it had no nose, so it helped me push the trash to the corner on Thursday nights.

My sphinx ate only cornflakes. It didn't care for bananas or ice cream or boiled ham or noodle soup, so I kept its bowl full beside the back door and made sure it had enough water. It spent a good deal of time staring at the cars that drove by my house and sharpening its claws on the maple tree. When it shat little piles of sand all over the lawn I was a bit annoyed, but the sand smelled only of sand so I didn't think it would be a bother.

"It's going to kill the grass," said my boyfriend as we ate dinner and watched the sphinx chase squirrels outside.

"It just has to get the desert out of its system," I said. "Spending a few thousand years there is bound to create problems."

My boyfriend harrumphed. When we'd started dating three years earlier he said he loved me because I was smart and compassionate and good at remembering things like dental appointments and when to pay the credit card bill. I liked that he was kind and easygoing and good at calming me down when I got anxious, but when he kept forgetting to lock the door I started to wonder if he was more lazy than laid-back. He worked in a bank. He was supposed to understand the importance of locks. Still, he had a point about the grass, so I made sure to spread the sand around the lawn before he came home.

My sphinx was quite tidy, regularly cleaned itself with its pink tongue, which I discovered was rough like a cat's because I let it lick me once and thought it was going to take the skin off my whole hand. Sometime my sphinx was a little overprotective. It stayed close to me outside and growled when the mail carrier came near, but it recognized its territory and never strayed over the property line. There was a certain grace to the sphinx, a certain power and intelligence in those eyes. Difficult to resist.

The lady across the street was jealous, said she knew of this place out in Wyoming, a unicorn ranch, and she was going to send for one as soon as she had the money.

"I'm going to buy a mare," she told me while standing beside the curb and eyeing my sphinx. "A white one with a beautiful horn. I've heard they eat a lot of grass so I won't have to mow the lawn once it arrives, but they like to rub their horns against trees and that can take all the bark off, so you need to provide them with an alternate horn-sharpening post."

My maple tree was showing signs of wear from the sphinx's claws, so I knew this was the sort of thing I should consider, but when I gave the sphinx a two-by-four it just kept using the tree. I acquiesced and sacrificed the maple because I wanted it to be happy.

During the day I sat in the insurance office, answered the phone and filled out paperwork and got quotes and asked clients to please have a seat in the waiting room. I knew all about house fires, car crashes, tornadoes, and floods, as well as accidents people could have with electrical cords, trees, cutlery, and swimming pools.

Sometimes there wasn't much to talk about with a client while she waited, so she told me the details of the horrific thing that had recently befallen this uninsured friend or family member, which was why she had to ease her new anxiety with several thousand dollars' worth of coverage. I did not explain that I had eased my own anxieties with a sphinx because I didn't want to start a trend.

After work I liked leaning against the sphinx, listening to the beat of its centuries-old heart, because it seemed reliable. I didn't have to wait for my boyfriend to get home so I could tell him about my day. I could tell the sphinx. This was a much better arrangement since I didn't get upset when my boyfriend went for an after-work drink with the other bank tellers. While he got bored with my insurance office stories and said they all sounded the same, the sphinx looked at me with sympathy and licked its paw.

Like all loving pets, the sphinx left gifts on the back porch. A mouse with the head of a bird. A bird with the head of a mouse. Once or twice a large black raven.

"This is disgusting," said my boyfriend when the sphinx left a sparrow with the head of a snake outside the glass door that led to the patio.

And perhaps it was, but the neighbors didn't complain about the sphinx, and I didn't notice a decrease in the number of songbirds. The burglar who'd been prowling the area was found lying under our across-the-street neighbor's dining room window with several abrasions, a few cuts on his face, and a broken arm. He did not, maybe could not, explain what happened when the police came, just handed over several pocketfuls of jewelry and asked for medical attention. I hugged my sphinx and gave it extra cornflakes.

"If I'd had my unicorn, those thefts would have stopped earlier," said my across-the-street neighbor, though she brought over a box of cornflakes for my sphinx to show her gratitude. The sphinx grimaced at her, but she kept close to the curb.

Following that incident there were calls from the authorities, some questioning if I'd acquired my sphinx through legal means, but I had all the necessary importation documents and a bill of sale. The sphinx was well-mannered around the police, knew to respect authority figures, so after inspecting my paperwork the police went on their way.

The sphinx usually sat stern and sentry-still in front of my house. Sometimes it eyed passersby in a menacing fashion, but they stayed on the sidewalk and everything was fine. When I got home it almost pounced on me, happy for something else to guard. It growled at my boyfriend when he arrived at eight in the evening.

"It's vicious," he grumbled.

"You're late," I said.

"I stayed a little long at happy hour," he said. "I needed to relax."

We didn't do that in the same way anymore.

My boyfriend said he'd make dinner, so while he was cooking I played catch with the sphinx, threw a big rubber hot dog that the sphinx brought back to me in its mouth. The hot dog was its favorite toy, maybe because it was long and thin and kind of mummy-shaped.

"It's going to hurt some kid," said my boyfriend.

"It is not," I said. The sphinx could tell a threat from an annoying brat and acted accordingly. "It only attacks prowlers. And it makes me feel better when you're not here."

"Come to dinner with me and some of the other guys from the bank," he said.

"I'm too tired," I said.

"You're no fun," he said.

"Try working in my insurance office all day and see how much you feel like going out afterwards," I said.

My boyfriend told me I was too damn sensitive for my own good.

A month later the sphinx became ill and spit up grit all over the place. I called off work and sat with it in the backyard, trying to feed it bananas because I knew they were good for upset stomachs. The sphinx ate a little to make me happy, but I could tell it didn't like the taste. Still, my sphinx cheered to be near me, and I wondered if its sickness had to do with heartache and missing the desert. I slept outside with the sphinx every other night so it would quit its mournful howling.

"You can't mother it all the time," said my boyfriend. "It will only get more needy."

"Maybe it's homesick," I said. "It might need a few more weeks to get over that. You could come sleep with us. You always liked camping."

"I'll stay inside," he said. "But I miss you in bed."

I muttered that he shouldn't be the one to complain since he was out till two on the weekend.

Everything was fine for a month and a half until I heard a roar while I was setting the table for dinner. By the time I came outside my sphinx was sitting beside the front door looking placid.

A neighborhood mother raged across the street ten minutes later.

"Your sphinx tried to tear my son apart," she said, "then it dragged him across the street to my house."

I told her my sphinx was a guard, wouldn't bother her son as long as he behaved himself.

She called the police anyway, said the sphinx had her son's shirt collar in its mouth.

"The sphinx tried to kill me," whined the kid and showed the officers his scraped knees, but they were nothing worse than he'd get if he fell down on the pavement.

I worried about a citation or worse—they might take the sphinx away from me—but my neighbor who wanted the unicorn tromped across the street, yelling that she'd seen the kid standing in the middle of my lawn throwing rocks at my sphinx and hitting it with a stick. One of the policemen knew the kid had a few misdemeanors involving bricks and store windows. Because the kid had been trespassing on my property, the police let me go with a warning to keep the sphinx chained in my yard at least ten feet away from the sidewalk. I agreed without much hesitation. My sphinx could break any restraint if my house were really threatened.

"This is crazy," said my boyfriend when he got home and found the police cruiser parked in the street outside our house.

"I'll keep the sphinx chained," I said. "It will be fine."

"Until the sphinx kills that kid," he said.

"It just scratched him up," I said. "It didn't even kill the burglar."

"This is crazy," my boyfriend said again.

But I needed the sphinx, especially after eight hours at work, the blur of claims and disaster stories that left me frazzled. The thought of my sphinx waiting by the garage was a comfort. I knew it would bite any intruder, warn me of any fire, be steady even in tornado winds, but the poor thing kept whining at the back door, asking to be let in the house. I sighed, went outside and sat with it on the step thinking of how pharaohs never had to deal with such problems.

To his credit my boyfriend never said "Either the sphinx goes or I do." The breakup had been coming for a while. We never spent time together. We had different ideas of fun. The sphinx only sped the inevitable. I sat with it by the garage while my boyfriend loaded cardboard boxes in his car. We managed to shake hands before he left. The sphinx didn't growl. It knew when I needed to be protected and when I didn't.

That night I tried to fit the sphinx inside the house, shoved it through the back door. It had to stay in the kitchen because its shoulders were too wide to go through any other door, but I got a plastic bucket from the garage so the sphinx could do its business inside. It was a pain to get the sphinx out of the house again the next morning. It didn't want to go and left claw marks on the kitchen floor.

The sphinx walked beside me to the back door when I came home from work, rubbed against me pleadingly, but I had to shake my head no. Those claw marks were never going to come out of the linoleum. I felt bad leaving the sphinx out-side, but I slept with it in the garage. I was lonely, too. When I lay beside the sphinx I hoped I would dream of pyramids and parades they had for the pharaohs when they died, but I only had nightmares about car accidents and house fires, accidents I couldn't prevent. When I woke up shivering I put my arm over the sphinx. It snuggled against me and purred until I fell asleep again, lulled by that soft rumble.

By late fall my sphinx lay beside its bowl of cornflakes without eating, and no longer tumbled after red and orange and yellow leaves. I worried, unsure who I should call because this wasn't the sort of problem I could take to the vet. I hadn't thought the sphinx would mind being away from Egypt. It was used to staying in one place and happy to guard things. I'd been told the sphinx came willingly, hopped right off its pedestal, but those had been the words of a salesman.

The sphinx started acting out, sulking by the holly bush and growling at small dogs, but it seemed remorseful after I scolded it for pouncing on the mail carrier and scratching his arms. It hid in the backyard while I went to find the disinfectant, apologizing to the mail carrier all the way.

"I don't know what got into it," I said. "It's never done that before."

I sat with the sphinx after dinner, brushed the sand out of its coat, shook my head. It licked my hand, a kiss like sandpaper.

The day after that, the sphinx was gone. I'm not sure where. I left out bowls of cornflakes but they remained full. I wasn't as sad as I thought I might be since I knew the sphinx had not been happy, and depressed sphinxes might not make good guards.

After it left, my old nighttime anxiety returned. I still hated being alone. Every creak made me start. I installed a deadbolt and chain in the front and back doors. I tried to stop watching the evening news on the advice of my next-door neighbor who was an elementary school guidance counselor, though sometimes I couldn't fall asleep until one in the morning.

There were other things I considered to alleviate my nervousness. I thought about quitting my job, finding one that was less stressful. I thought about going to group therapy since there had to be other people with the same problem.

Then the lady across the street reminded me that sphinxes hadn't worked for the pharaohs, either, since they had all their treasure stolen and put in museums.

"I'm going to order my unicorn next week," she said.

I wondered if that might be a good idea. Easier than quitting my job, and big groups made me shy. I wasn't very good at talking about myself in front of other people. Besides, unicorns were pretty and would look nice in the yard.

The Dreamlords

WE LIVED WITH my father in a two-bedroom house that had once seemed too small, then became too big. Or maybe I was so accustomed to being cramped that extra space felt excessive, made me aware of the absence of my mother and husband and how my daughter had once slept on the couch but now had a small bed in my room. She was eight and in third grade, a bright kid who liked drawing and carefully ignored the fact that we bought clothes from garage sales.

"It's more fun this way," she said when we scoured someone else's card tables for sweatshirts and jeans in her size. Like any eight-year-old it seemed she'd sprouted another inch every time I turned around. She looked for shirts with bright colors and sparkles. I squinted at the fabric to be certain there were no stains I couldn't get out with a good scrub.

But my daughter was clean, warm, and fed, which had been tricky before I had the dreaming job, especially when we needed extra money to repair the house. My husband had done that when he was alive, and now that he'd been gone for two years, there were window drafts he would have patched, but I couldn't. My dad didn't have the stamina to carry my husband's heavy toolbox, and I worried about him with the electric drill. Even mopping the kitchen left him breathless at the table. I sewed curtains and made doorstops to keep out the cold, but it was my dreaming that bought us new windows. That helped a lot, especially during winter.

I was lucky that my kid loved drawing. It was entertaining and cheap.

"I'm going to be an architect when I grow up," she told me when showing off her latest artwork. "Like Daddy wanted to do."

I adjusted my glasses and held the drawing closer to see the pointed conical roofs that reminded me of unicorn horns. Her father had drawn fanciful castles, telling her tales about the people who lived inside. He loved the delicate puzzle of buildings, of stonework techniques and steel skeletons beneath cement and glass.

"When we have enough money, I'll go back to school," he often said. I tried to add to our savings, but we always had some more pressing financial need. Leaky roof. Leaky pipes. Broken water heater. But I still saw his cities in my dreams: their twisting stairways, turreted towers, and grinning gargoyles nested in my mind. That might have explained the high demand. Often my dreams were copied and sold over and over to various clients.

I ENTERED THE dream business simply enough, when I was chatting with the wife of one of the dreamlords. She was a regular customer at the salon where I worked doing hair and nails, trying to make enough to pay the rent on my booth and eat. She liked my manicures, the delicate flowers, polka dots, and other patterns I painted on her nails. With creativity like that, she told me, I might have a talent for dreaming.

"It's easy money, dear," she said, admiring her hands as I started her pedicure. "All you do is go to work and go to sleep."

But like many things that people claim are easy, it was the hardest job of my life.

The problem was I was good at it, an effective and prolific dreamer, but that was part of the dreamlords' business plan— find employees when they're young and proceed to wring their brains dry of color.

I made a good wage, a really good wage, more than my parents' combined salary at the auto factory. The working conditions were nice. The room had twenty beds, and smelled of lavender or lilac. The beds had just enough give to the mattress, more comfortable than my bed at home, except that my head rested in a helmet-like hollow, held in place on either side by a firm pillow. My mind was scanned for approximately seven and a half hours a day. Then I was awakened along with the other dreamers, the attendants changed the covers on our beds, and the next shift came in. They gave us a snack before we went to sleep, and a meal when we woke.

After a shift I was blinking and groggy for a few minutes—it took longer to wake up than from normal sleep—and sometimes I felt dizzy as the machines whirred to a stop. Their buzz reminded me of restless bees. I imagined them flying into my ears and whirling around my head, then speeding out again. The echo of wings never quite left my mind.

And I was hungry. Always hungry. It might have been a side effect of the dream enhancement drugs they gave us at work, but we ate well. A thick layer of cheese on the lasagna, the best chicken parmesan I'd ever tasted, real butter on the noodles, and fresh steamed vegetables. The dreamlords hired gourmet chefs to prepare all our meals: one of the tiny perks to maintain the illusion that our bosses cared.

The dreamlord's wife often hovered around the cafeteria chatting with dreamers.

"I never had food like this before," Angela told her as we ate baked ziti, or chicken amandine, or beef bourguignon. The dreamlord's wife would nod, smile, and float away.

Usually Angela had two helpings of whatever we were eating, but she was so thin I knew she needed it. Every day after work she gave me a sleep-slow smile and said she'd see me tomorrow. She was going home to take a nap.

Dream-sleep was far from restful. The scanners invaded my head, recording full-length dreams as well as scraps of ideas and images. Often I dreamed of riding a horse through green fields, toward a Gothic building with spires that grazed the sky. Sometimes I was being chased by furies—monsters with the heads of women and bodies of huge black birds—and the castle was my refuge. Other times I wandered its halls looking for my husband, poking my head in each room and noting the tapestries and gold-framed oil paintings. My mind had a flair for medieval romance, I suppose, though in most dreams I was caught between anticipation and annoyance because I knew my husband was hiding from me.

I didn't know why my dreams were so popular with a certain clientele, though I assume it had to do with the stunning architecture and the love they might have had for horses. I'd never ridden a horse, but I dreamed it convincingly enough. Other times I dreamed a volcano had sprouted in the middle of Main Street, spewing lava and ash. I was running home to grab my daughter. I didn't know where we would go, just that I had to find her and my dad. Nobody told me whether those end-of-time dreams were popular, but I suppose they appealed to a certain market. Everything did.

Often I came home with a buzzing headache, my mind full of after-images, the things and people from my dreams infiltrating my waking hours.

MY MOTHER HAD worked in the same auto factory as my dad, but her lungs gave out before his, wheezing and on oxygen. My husband had worked in construction and suffered a heart attack on the job, too obstinate to admit that there might be a problem lurking in his chest pains. He was thirty-five, and he'd been having those pains for a while. He joked it was my cooking. I told him to see a doctor. He said, "With what money?" And he was too young for anyone to consider his heart.

Six months after I started dream work, both of them were back in my life.

"We need more tomato sauce," my mother said as I made dinner. She'd been gone for five years, but I dreamed her often.

"The bridge is coming down!" the mayor yelled as he streaked through the hallway toward the living room. At work that day I'd dreamed town had been hit by a meteor, an interesting variant on my destruction-of-everything-by-fiery-lava-flow dream.

"You have to think about your vision," said my dead husband, leaning against the counter with his arms crossed. "And your visions."

"I have," I said. "I'm not quitting the job." Since birth I'd been legally blind without glasses. My prescription was the sort that gave everyone else headaches, but since I'd started dreaming, the world had grown hazier. My daughter's features were slightly blurred. Words on street signs were fuzzy. Who knew how long before I wouldn't be able to read them at all.

"Some sacrifices aren't worth it," said my husband, but he didn't have to worry about buying food or covering the mortgage and utilities. I knew I looked like shit. I wished I could have afforded the fancy dream-recording equipment to launch my own business, but I couldn't even buy dream-enhancement supplements. Those were a couple of pills we dreamers swallowed before going to sleep. The chemicals danced with the ones in our brains to make our dreams more vivid, both when we were asleep and when we were awake. My husband looked so real standing in the kitchen that I asked him to hand me the salt shaker.

"Can't help you there," he said, smirking as he stepped to one side.

"Asshole," I muttered. Perhaps it was wrong to curse the dead, but I figured it was okay when engaged in two-way conversation. It was an odd kindness that he didn't make me grab for the shaker by reaching through his body. He'd always been a tease.

I WANTED TO send my daughter to a school where she could focus on her art, but I worried the dreamlords would have their eyes on her. I still felt the gaze of the dreamlord's wife when she skirted around the edges of the cafeteria. Maybe it was the lack of sleep that bred my paranoia. Maybe I was right to feel paranoid. The dreamlords were predatory. They took the bright ones, the imaginative ones, tracking their test scores through junior high and high school. At least according to Angela, and I had no reason to disbelieve her. She said kids who seemed particularly creative were invited to apply for a position even before graduation. That's what had happened to her and a couple of her friends. After a night or two in a scanner, they were offered jobs, lucrative ones. Hard for any smart kid to say no when the alternative was college debt.

"My mom was so happy about it," Angela told me more than once. "She worried that I'd have a hard time getting a job since I'd always had my head in the clouds."

A lot of the dreamers—Angela and I included—were the highest wage earners in our families, but power and pressure came with that salary. Angela lived with her mother, who worked the night shift at a bakery and brought home two-day-old bread. She earned more than three times as much as her mom, and only told me that every other week.

Dreamers rarely left the profession. We needed the paycheck. We loved the food. But there were other reasons that we didn't talk about. Weaning yourself off dream-enhancement supplements was awful. The withdrawal period involved migraines and paranoia, something the dreamlords didn't admit, but people who'd been off work for more than four days due to illness said it was better to go in and dream when you were half-dead than try to cope without drugs.

BEFORE I STARTED dreaming professionally, I'd never imagined walking through my husband's buildings. With the enhancement supplements, those structures took on a three-dimensional quality that stunned me. The furniture. The chandeliers. The string quintet in the ballroom playing baroque music. This was as close as I came to entering his mind, and for that I was willing to put up with the gargoyles that had detached themselves from the outside walls and proceeded to track mud on the paisley carpets. I chased them down long halls while my husband ran after me, laughing, telling me I shouldn't worry. It was just a stupid rug, after all.

He caught me from behind, squeezing me in a hug.

"You're too uptight," he said. "Gargoyles will be gargoyles."

"You'd give them the run of this place if I wasn't here," I said.

"Probably," he said, letting go and turning me around for a kiss.

It was good to kiss my husband, to hug my husband, even in that dream space, but I paid a price. There was the constant tiredness, the blankness when making dinner that led me to burn the hamburgers more than once.

"At least we have something to eat," said my father when I presented another round of charcoal briquettes on buns.

"I like my burgers well-done," said my daughter. I preferred medium rare.

"We're much better off than we used to be," my father said, coughing twice and then patting my fingers. I barely felt his touch. My plate appeared in triplicate, and I had to slide my hand along the table to figure out which one was real. If they noticed anything wrong, my father and daughter didn't say so.

AFTER DINNER, I sat beside my daughter on the couch to watch TV while she drew. I squinted, pressing my glasses closer to my face to see what she was sketching. Green fields with a tiny gray blob in the distance.

"In art class we're working on perspective," she said. "Do you like the castle? I had to make it really small."

"Beautiful," I said. My husband sat across the room in his usual chair, wearing the watch I gave him for our first wedding anniversary. "You're going to be a great architect someday." I'd started saving for her college; I wanted to cement that dream in my daughter's head, so she'd never take those tests at school. I would keep her home sick on test days.

THE ANNOYING PART was when the nightmares followed me into the kitchen or grocery store, where I saw gargoyles among the cornflakes in aisle six. I knew they weren't real because they stood out more clearly than the surrounding boxes. I squinted to make sure I was buying the honey nut and not apple cinnamon cereal, and brushed a gargoyle to one side as it tried to bite my hand.

"Why did you draw so many damn gargoyles?" I asked my husband on the drive home, craning my neck to peer over two of them as they danced across the dashboard. After I batted them away, they turned a few somersaults to show me they didn't care about abuse.

"You always said they were cute," he said in the passenger seat.

"That was when they had smaller fangs and didn't climb on everything," I said.

"They like heights," he said.

"You always take their side," I said. My husband grinned and kissed my cheek. I tried to remember the feeling of pressure as his lips brushed my skin.

THE DREAMLORDS WANTED bad dreams as well as good ones. Our supervisors at work explained it with a shrug, saying some customers had nightmare fetishes. It wasn't our job to question taste. But the rumor among us dreamers was that our terrors were used for extortion. Nobody knew how the dreamlords would do that—their clients used helmet-like dream-transferal devices similar to our dream-scanners—but our cafeteria chatter was rampant with whispered conjectures on how the dreamlords could bypass that technology. Strung-out dreamers high on cash and caffeine and who knows what other drugs would believe anything.

"They're going to weaponize our dreams," Angela told me at dinner with a conspiratorial smile. "I heard they're working with the government to develop dream bombs. They could terrorize armies or whole countries, make them all sleepless so they surrender with nobody dying." She winked at me like we were in on it. I nodded and took another bite of lasagna. I didn't think the dreamlords could manufacture missiles from our haunts and fears, but that didn't stop workplace speculation.

"It's a bunch of horseshit," said my husband as he played with the straw in my drink. "Your friend is too far gone." It was difficult not to respond to him, to remember which voices were in which world. I could only talk back at home, but in the cafeteria it was hard to get him to shut up. I smiled and nodded at Angela, and wondered how much longer we'd be working together.

Exhaustion wasn't the only side effect of dreaming. Some of the dreamers, the really good ones, had been hospitalized for prolonged periods of time. Some of them never came out. Calvin who dreamed of dragons had dissolved behind the walls of an institution. So had Sylvia who dreamed of flying, and Edmond who always fell off cliffs. Maybe they were admitted because of headaches. Or hallucinations. Or some other malady I hadn't yet experienced. But that didn't matter. After my daughter went to bed, my father noticed me rubbing my temples. Another eye-strain headache.

"You should quit if you need to," he said, but his voice was strained. He'd left his job six years ago after decades as a car spray painter gave him a permanent wheeze. The insurance at my dreaming job paid for treatments we could never afford before, but even so, doing two loads of laundry wore him out for the day. Everyone in my family had sacrificed themselves for their paychecks. I never thought to question it, but even if I had, I might not have arrived at a different answer.

MY MOST FREQUENT nightmare was of my husband being crushed under wooden beams at a construction site. In the dream I sprinted down the street, thinking I could save him if I got there soon enough. I woke up panting. Sometimes my husband was sitting beside me in bed.

"The bad one again," he said, lifting his hand to tuck a lock of hair behind my ear. I couldn't feel his touch, but that didn't stop him from hugging me, slipping his body through the sheets and under my nightgown. One time we made love, though that might have been a dream. I don't remember worrying that our daughter was in the room, just that I arched my back when I gasped into climax, and closed my eyes. When I opened them the room was gray with morning.

Other times, most times, when I woke after the nightmare, my husband wasn't there. It took forever to find sleep again. In my waking hours I came home to gargoyles ransacking the kitchen. They dumped a gallon of milk on the floor, squished their feet in the butter, and did a jig on sugar cookies scattered across the counter.

"I don't need this stress," I told my husband. In the hallway another gargoyle was ripping up my favorite blouse. Even if I knew it wasn't real—the cookie crumbs and smears of butter were too clearly defined against the haze of the wood grain—it still raised my blood pressure.

"Just a dream," he said, patting my shoulder. "But I can't stop them."

I wanted the impossible, for my husband to have never drawn gargoyles or died in the first place, though I couldn't do anything about either situation and resorted to slamming drawers and cupboards while I made macaroni and cheese. We had the same arguments over and over, stuck at the point in time when he'd left.

"You should open a new salon, your own place," he said.

"We'd lose our secondhand shirts," I said.

"Would you rather lose that or your mind?" he said as I wrinkled my nose and took the boiling pasta off the stove. I tapped the side of the pot against the colander in the sink to make sure it was really there.

My husband cleared his throat. "I don't want you to keep dreaming. She'll lose you, too."

I banged the empty pot back on the stove. "I'll be fine," I said. At dinner I asked my father to drive me to work, saying he might as well use the car during the day. His spectral form nodded. My hazy pink-shirted daughter glanced from him to me.

My family was turning into ghosts as my husband stood in a corner of the kitchen and shook his head. Was this a choice I really wanted to make? The thought made me dizzy. Ditzy. Muddled. That's why I wasn't in my right mind when I wondered aloud to Angela as we ate dinner the next day.

"Sometimes I don't know how much longer I can keep doing this."

She nodded. She understood. But I should have had my half wits about me. I should have known other people could be listening. The following day the dreamlord's wife came over while I had my morning snack.

"I hear you're thinking about leaving us," she said, her voice light as she gripped the back of a chair.

"Not really," I said, picking grapes off the stem. "It's hard to find good jobs."

"My thoughts exactly," she said. "How will you feed your child?"

"How will you protect your sanity?" said my husband, who sat beside me.

I patted my lips with a napkin. "I suppose it's time to get to work."

MY DAUGHTER APPEARED beside my bed that night, though it took a moment to determine that she was real.

"I had a bad dream," she said. I let her climb in with me, but I wasn't really awake until she started explaining the dream. No, it was a nightmare. My nightmare. The similarities were uncanny. She saw her father dragging a beam from the back of a truck, and the avalanche of wood from the truck bed crushing his chest, a scene I'd dreamed many times but never told her.

"You were running down the street to get to him," she said.

I hugged her tight. "Just a dream," I said. Even inches from my face, her features blurred. When I turned my head I saw my husband lying next to me, every eyebrow and eyelash clearly defined. He wrapped his arms around both of us.

I was exhausted and unable to sleep. I didn't want to believe the rumors that the dreamlords could beam dreams into people's heads from a distance.

But maybe my daughter's nightmare didn't come from them. There were other rumors about how dreamers developed skills nobody could prove but everyone half believed, like how we could project dreams. The theory was that dream-extracting machines and the dream-enhancement drugs opened up other pathways in our minds. When Angela gossiped about the notion, I had thought it was a load of crap, but after my daughter had dreams that were so close to mine... Was it me? The dreamlords? Coincidence?

As I made breakfast, my husband sat on the counter and my mother stood beside him. A gargoyle toddled across the floor at her feet, trailing a roll of toilet paper. Two more gargoyles played soccer with a lemon.

"The dreamlords can't send nightmares," said my husband. "It's a load of horseshit."

"I wouldn't underestimate them," said my mother. "And you're out of coffee."

The gargoyles kicked the lemon into the sink.

Yes, it seemed impossible, but I worried when my daughter had nightmares a second night in a row. A third. A fourth. Always showing up at my bedside, asking to sleep with me. I couldn't refuse, worried that her artist's mind was too vulnerable to dream intrusion.

Following the fourth nightmare, I found her napping on the couch after school. She hadn't slept well. My husband stood beside her, brushing his fingers over the brown fog of her hair. I had to do something, no matter how small and speculative. I had to try sending good dreams to her and supplant the bad.

That evening after she was in bed and I heard the soft rhythm of her breath, I sat on the edge of my mattress with my hands on my knees, matching my inhale and exhale to hers. I imagined a violet stream arching from my head across the room to her forehead. I pictured the winding staircases of her father's castles, a stray gargoyle scampering across the stone hallways. Outside the castle two gargoyles ran through a field of tulips, grinning bright-toothed smiles and eating flowers. She'd always liked gargoyles. They made her laugh. When I cut the dream off, I envisioned a swirl like water going down the drain, the tail of the dream spinning through the air between us.

Then I imagined the dreamlord's wife in her cavernous house. The dreamlords all had cavernous houses, ones built from the bricks of our nightmares and reveries. I didn't pause to think deeply about consequences, whether she could have some terror sent to me if she determined who'd plagued her with bad dreams. I pictured the charcoal gray arc from my mind to hers, her lips pursed as she dreamed herself driving alone on a long stretch of road, blank fields on either side, and deep ditches without guardrails for protection. At an intersection an approaching car tried to brake but skidded forward. Her hands gripped the steering wheel, tried to swerve away from the jolt of impact, her mouth opening to scream—

The next scene, a steel and glass office building with fingers of smoke curling from the windows, the dreamlord's wife running down the street. Her husband was inside, on the tenth floor, a faceless man prying at one of the closed windows. There was nothing in his office heavy enough to break the glass. He tried his desk chair. The window did not yield. His eyes burned. Her eyes burned. She coughed with smoke, ran toward the lobby entrance but invisible arms grabbed her shoulders, held her back, a man's voice yelled it was too dangerous. She couldn't wrest herself from his grip. Fire broke a window. Orange tongues licked the air—

I opened my eyes to the gray bedroom. Maybe I shouldn't have acted on the whim, but it was too easy. I pictured her sitting up in bed, blinking in darkness, the odor of smoke still in her nose. When I lay down I went to sleep in moments, though I saw my husband perched on my dresser, mumbling about how there was something very wrong with all this.

But my bright and blurry daughter didn't visit my bedside all night. I didn't see the dreamlord's wife in the cafeteria the next day. Or the day after that. I felt triumphant and even shittier than before, though there were no results from the experiment that I could verify, other than my husband sitting next to me in the cafeteria saying "Honey, this is wearing you out."

I didn't disagree, but there were benefits to losing my mind and sight simultaneously. I was learning how to cook by touch, using my fingers to tell when a measuring cup was full, and curling them back to guide the blade of the knife when I chopped vegetables. Sight wasn't reliable, but I started to care less about that as the two worlds blurred.

Everything in my dream's eye view might as well be what was in reality. Maybe that was indeed the truth, and what most people called going crazy was actually gaining clarity. I'm sure someone had said that before, since dreams clearly existed in the world of your mind, which was equally important to the waking world. Why maintain a hierarchy? What was wrong with a world in which everyone could still be alive? Most people didn't have a choice in that matter.

At work Angela was grumbling again about how her mother just didn't understand the seriousness of our work and how it could be so draining.

"She doesn't understand why I can't keep my eyes open and have dinner," said Angela, "but when I get home I'm beat. Besides, sleep is so interesting now. I learn so many things about, you know, the universe."

"Like what?" I said, because even though we talked about our families, we never said much about our dreams.

She yawned and smiled. "I'll tell you tomorrow." But she didn't come in the next day, or the next. After four days, I told myself she was taking a little break, and continued to argue with my mother and husband when they lectured me in the kitchen.

"I'm dead," my husband said. "You know I'm dead."

"I am, too, honey," said my mother.

The gargoyles played in the coffee canister. The mayor sat at the kitchen table and sipped a cup of tea, waiting for the next tragedy to befall town.

"You're not dead in my dreams," I said.

"You're impossible," said my husband. The gargoyles sprinkled coffee beans across the linoleum, but I was getting used to having them around, and anyway I had to make dinner.

The Hostage

I DIDN'T THINK it was just my cat, it was breaking glass, then footfalls in the hall and the guy wearing all black standing in my living room with a knife.

"Hi," I said. "You know I have the disease." It was somewhat obvious since I had no eyebrows and hadn't painted them on yet that morning, but I made a point of telling people about the disease up front, regardless of whether they'd just broken into my house. If I wasn't straightforward, some tended to get irked.

"That's why I'm taking you hostage," he said. "Stay where you are."

But what was the fun in that? He backed up a little when I stood up from the couch and walked toward him. My hands were shaking, but his were shaking more. We talked about these kinds of people in my weekly support group, ones who believed the myths about us. He wouldn't want me to approach him, so that seemed like the most logical thing to do.

"Come on," I said, "you don't really want to take me hostage."

"Yes I do," he said and raised the knife a little, but his wrist was limp. I thought about chasing him out of the house so I could resume the morning, but friends from my support group lived a few blocks away. Lists of our addresses circulated online—it should have been illegal but wasn't—so we weren't that hard to find. I didn't want them to have to deal with him, especially not Laurie, who'd just come out of a real health scare.

"Put the knife down," I said. "We should talk."

"Talk about what?" he said. He couldn't even hide the tremble in his voice.

"What do you need to talk about?" I said. Shit, anyone who'd break into my house with a knife needed to talk about something. My nurse's training was helpful in this regard, since I knew how to manage traumatic situations: Be calm, take charge, don't overreact. The knife guy's eyes were darting around like a cornered rabbit. I realized I was blocking his escape route to the broken window. When I was four feet away he dropped the knife, which left both of us scrambling for it on the carpet. Because he backed away from me so easily, I won.

"I'm going to call the police," I said, walking toward him.

"Don't come any closer," he said, his voice cracking.

"You can have a seat," I said, gesturing to the couch with the pointy end of the knife.

He edged along the wall, being careful, I noticed, not to actually touch it.

"That's okay," he said, "I'll stand." I'm sure he was afraid my sofa was diseased. I didn't need any weapon other than being alive and in the same room.

"Suit yourself," I said, picking up the phone as I kept my eye on him.

He tugged at his black gloves as I listened to the phone ring on the other end of the line and made an effort not to laugh. When I was merely a theoretical diseased person he was all bravado and hostage-taking, but seeing me was different. I was curious what he'd planned to do. Use me as a biological weapon, perhaps threatening to make me spit on people? You couldn't transfer the disease that way, but I'd heard a few whack jobs on late-night TV talking about how folks like me could become lethal if we got pissed, and theoretically take out a whole neighborhood by shooting spitwads at passersby from our front porches. Most people scoffed at the idea of such plots. At least in public. I wondered if I should hiss a few times to see if he might piss his pants, but the dispatcher answered and I had to sound professional and explain my hostage and the disease.

"Are you in immediate danger?" the dispatcher asked, probably because I sounded calm.

"I've got things under control," I said.

"We'll send someone over soon," she said. "But there might be a little delay. Everyone on duty is already out on a call."

I didn't know whether this was the truth, but decided to believe her.

"It's okay," I said. "I offered him a seat."

She hung up and I was left with the quivering guy in black. Criminals weren't the sharpest pencils in the mug, and sometimes the mythology surrounding my condition was helpful, like now, when I told him to stand against the wall and keep quiet or I'd touch him. He did as I asked, just as my rather vocal cat decided to appear from wherever she'd been sleeping and start rubbing against his legs, meowing.

"She wants to be petted," I said.

"I'm allergic," he said.

"Guess you chose the wrong house," I said. I grabbed her bag of treats from the coffee table and shook it, and she rapidly shifted alliances. My hostage, as I was now affectionately calling him, relaxed his shoulders slightly. Sadly he was not a real hostage since I didn't know who would pay money to get him back. We were simply hostage to each other's morning schedules, and he was hostage to his fear of a lethal spitwad.

I was curious about him, since I'd never talked with one of these fanatics, just heard stories. They rarely got close enough to us to have an actual conversation. The hostage story wasn't new—people had invaded the homes of those with the disease before, spouting grand plans to poison the water supply or taint buffets at restaurants with our bodily fluids. The perpetrators were arrested and taken in for mental health evaluations.

"What did you want to do with me anyway," I said, "after taking me hostage?"

"I don't know," he mumbled.

"Do you have syringes?" I asked, trying to add an edge to my voice. "I don't want to pat you down, but—"

"Okay, maybe I was going to take some blood," he said.

"And do what?"

"I don't know. Like, times are rough. I'm barely making rent." He peered around my living room squint-eyed like he was resenting it. Why would someone with the disease have nice things and gainful employment? I wondered if that was part of the anger against us. Diseased people should not have good jobs, or cars, or even be mobile. We needed to be in an area set off from the rest of society.

Most people said they weren't scared of contracting the disease, but you never knew who might be standing next to you in the grocery line and freak out if you had no eyebrows.

Eyebrow loss was one of the first symptoms of the disease, in addition to a slightly higher white blood cell count, and an occasional persistent sneeze. That was stage one. Stage two was an even higher white blood cell count, hazy vision, dilated pupils, and increased blood pressure. Stage three was a heart attack. Stages two and three came within twenty-four hours of each other if you didn't get treatment right away to return to stage one. Like other blood-borne viruses it had spread quietly until there was a rash of heart attacks among young people who didn't have a family history of heart disease or high blood pressure. The discovery of a virus didn't still the panic for a couple of months until the means of transmission was confirmed, but in schools and workplaces some people still called for infected individuals to wear plastic gloves and use special bathrooms.

Everyone in my neighborhood was as kind and educated as anyone could be about the disease, but there was a couple who had moved out when they learned I was moving in. My next-door neighbor Vivian told me not to worry about it.

"I didn't like them anyway, honey," she said. "You just got rid of the riffraff."

I smiled and nodded, wondering how riffy and raffy the old neighbors had been. Those kinds of moves weren't rare, as I discovered in my support group. Everyone in the group had the disease, or had a family member with the disease. We met weekly at someone's house to bitch about the slow process of medical research, and to counsel each other.

"Other kids are still staying away from him," Melanie said last week. Her son Andrew had been diagnosed three months ago. "He has a couple of friends, I think their parents are doctors, but he wasn't invited to a birthday party this week with the other boys in his class. We went to see a movie, but he cried the whole afternoon."

Her voice cracked. Tina gave her a side hug. We all wanted hugs, human contact, reassurance that things would be okay, since we feared hidden symptoms and other long-term effects. Doctors couldn't figure out what they might be before they happened.

Some members of the group had been like me and worked in health care or other so-called "sensitive professions," but we'd been relocated, reassigned, or otherwise repositioned after our diagnosis so we wouldn't have direct physical contact with patients. Technically it was against the law to discriminate, so they found other names, such as strategic personnel rotation.

"If your patients found out you had the disease, they might feel hurt or betrayed," the office manager told me gently. "They could lash out. That's why we think this is best for all concerned." I gritted my teeth, accepted the new work-from-home assignment, and became determined to prove to the world that someone could have the disease and things would be fine, fine, fine.

But I did have a weird power over my hostage, like my finger was a gun loaded with blood, and all I had to do was prick it and tell him to bark like a dog. That's why I walked to the bathroom, grabbed a bottle of alcohol, a cotton swab, and a pin, and came back out. My hostage's eyes widened, and he shivered visibly. I felt alternately disgusted and dangerous.

"What are you going to do?" he said, trying not to let his voice shake and doing a very bad job of it.

"This is in case you misbehave," I said. "Please walk to the kitchen." I nodded at the door. Still quivering, he obeyed.

I wanted to follow through with my previous breakfast plans, so I flipped through my cookbooks for a gingerbread pancake recipe. I stood with my pin at the counter, still wearing my nightgown. I was not going to let him ruin my morning, but ended up paying more attention to my hostage than the cookbook as he squirmed and peered around my kitchen.

"Would you like pancakes?" I asked.

"I'm fine," he said.

"They're really good pancakes," I said. "Gingerbread pancakes. There's molasses, cinnamon, cloves, and ginger in the batter. I just have to find the recipe."

"I'm fine," he said again.

"Suit yourself." I hadn't had a meal with someone since the last group meeting. My cat was pleasant company, but not the best for dinner conversation.

I flipped another page in my cookbook and realized I hadn't checked my blood pressure that morning. There were days when I checked my blood pressure obsessively, every half hour, sure that I felt a little off and was going into stage two again. We'd lost two support group members since I'd joined, though I hadn't told my mother. Justin was younger than me, only twenty-two, and Angela was five years older, a mom with two kids. Both of them were on vacation, camping and hiking, but getting away from populated areas held a certain kind of danger. Angela and Justin loved the outdoors, said they were careful, and that they wouldn't let the disease stop them from living. They were both healthy and vibrant and listened to their bodies—another mantra of ours—then they were gone. That was where the contradictions came in, where all of us stood on the thin line between telling everyone they were safe and wouldn't catch the disease, and being very, very scared for our lives.

I'd called Melanie a few times at three in the morning to help me still a panic attack.

"You're not crazy for worrying," Melanie told me when I phoned her asking if I should buy an economy pack of plastic gloves. "Just take a deep breath."

"I feel like an idiot when I do this," I said, "but it's overwhelming."

"I might call you next week for the same reason," she said.

When the doorbell rang I remembered that Tina and Robert had promised to stop by and drop off the Tupperware bowl I'd brought to the last meeting with fruit salad. They'd made stew and wondered if I wanted some. My hostage stood up straight, ready to bolt, so I grabbed him by the arm, towed him to the door, unlocked it, and yelled "It's open!"

Then I dragged him to the living room so we could have a nice chat. I kept one hand on my hostage's upper arm as I gave Robert and Tina side hugs. "Sit down for a moment," I said. "I was going to make coffee."

"I had three cups already today," said Robert, "but we can stay for a few minutes. We're running errands."

"This is my new friend," I said, shoving my hostage forward as I maintained my vise grip. "He stopped by to learn about our condition."

Tina and Robert noticed his black attire. They smiled. They sat.

"It's nice when anyone reaches out to us," said Tina. "There are so many rumors going around about the condition."

"Uh-huh," said my hostage.

"I'm developing a curriculum for schools to educate children about people with the condition," said Tina. She and Robert never called it a disease. "There's so much misinformation going around, and you know how little kids can be cruel to each other when they're really just repeating things they've heard at home."

My hostage grunted.

"I'm hoping we can build a more understanding population while doctors keep searching for a cure," said Tina.

"Would you like a pamphlet?" said Robert, taking a stack of them out of his jacket pocket. "We're going to distribute it at local businesses."

"That's okay," said my hostage.

"You should come to our information night next week at the library," said Tina. "We're going to have a presentation on current research on the condition, and a Q and A."

"There should be a good turnout," I said.

My hostage looked at his shoes while Tina and Robert continued to chat about the library gathering and how nice it was that we could use the space for free since we were a community organization. They planned on buying donuts and having coffee so it would be a nice social event.

"The librarian has a nephew with the condition, so she understands," said Tina, leaning toward my hostage while he leaned back. "It's touched all of our friends and family members, so I don't know why the stigma is still so prevalent. That makes this kind of outreach even more important."

"Uh-huh," said my hostage. I think he was trying not to breathe.

Tina and Robert and I glanced at each other. They raised their eyebrows at me. I shrugged and nodded. Things were under control. They nodded back.

"Well, we have to get going," said Robert as he stood up, "but great to meet you."

He held out his hand for a shake.

"Sorry," said my hostage, "I've had a cold."

I gave Tina and Robert another side hug. They let themselves out and I locked the door, then put their stew in the fridge. I was going to resume looking through my cookbooks, but I was tired of listening to my hostage's nervous shuffle, and a donut sounded good. It didn't seem like the police would come soon—I doubted any officer would be eager for this kind of house call—and eventually my hostage would need to pee and wouldn't want to use my bathroom, so I'd have to take him to the backyard like a large dog. Or I could drive him to the police station before his bladder erupted.

But first I dragged him to the bathroom because I had to paint on my eyebrows. After months of practice I still hated doing it because I couldn't make myself symmetrical. The arcs were always too thin or uneven, but they made me appear slightly more normal if you didn't look too closely. I watched him in the mirror behind me, hands clasped and arms held tight to his body.

"How's this?" I asked, turning around to show off my new brows.

"Fine," he said, peering at his feet.

"You didn't even look," I said.

He gave me a half-second glance and returned his gaze to the floor. "Fine," he said.

I sighed, figuring that was the best I'd get, and hauled him back to the kitchen where I grabbed his knife, wrapped it in a lot of plastic wrap, and told him we were going to take a drive.

"I have to ride in your car?" he said.

"Shut up or I'll kiss you," I said, grabbing a denim jacket from the back of my chair and sliding shoes on my feet. Hopefully with the jacket, my nightgown would look like a pink cotton skirt. I directed him to the garage door and out to my car, where I had him sit in the front passenger seat.

"Keep your hands in your lap where I can see them," I said, and pushed the button to lock the doors. If he tried to escape I couldn't keep him confined, but he didn't like touching anything I might have touched. Getting to the police station would be a relief for us both, and until then I could take my time. I was still curious about him.

"Where are you from?" I asked as we backed out of my driveway.

"What?" he said.

"Where are you from?" I said.

"Oh," he said. "Cleveland. Just outside of Cleveland."

"Are your parents still there?"

"Mom is," he said, glancing at me. "Dad's dead."

"I'm sorry."

He shrugged. "Got to keep the repair shop going since it's mine now."

"Your dad started it?" I asked.

"Yeah," he said and looked out the window. "We worked together."

"Do you rebuild engines and transmissions and stuff?"

"Sometimes," he said.

"What does your mom do for a living?"

"School secretary," he said. "She's retired now. Has arthritis bad."

"So does my mom," I said. "Especially in her hands. She used to play piano a lot, but doesn't do that so much anymore."

I wondered if he'd ask me anything, but he didn't. Maybe he was scared. Or he didn't think I had a history. I was a disease. And he wanted out of this car.

That's why I stopped at the coffee shop drive-through for a vanilla latte.

"I thought we were going to the police station," he said.

"I need a latte," I said. "It's been a rough morning. Want anything?"

"I'm fine," he said.

"You're sure?" I said.

He gave me a tight nod, then I remembered I wanted donuts.

"Want to know how I got the disease?" I asked. He was silent. "It was when I was in the hospital getting my gall bladder out, and they took my appendix while they were at it. They gave me extra blood to make up for blood that I lost, then five years later, when I started feeling a little off and my eyebrows were thinning, I went in for an exam. They'd just discovered the disease then. You know that history." He probably didn't. "Most of the time I don't feel too bad. I only dipped into stage two once. That was scary, but then I went back up to stage one. Been that way ever since."

He stared out the front windshield. I wondered if it even mattered that I was talking.

"My mom freaked out because she'd heard the doom-and-gloom scenarios on the news," I said. "It took a while for her to understand that it wasn't as bad as some of the reports suggested." Mom was still researching homeopathic quack cures that she e-mailed to me with great regularity.

The boyfriend I'd had at the time of my diagnosis broke up with me six months later. He said it wasn't related to the disease. Sometimes I believed him. We'd always used protection since I didn't want to end up pregnant, but I was relieved when his test came back negative. Our sex life had been lackluster even before the diagnosis, the relationship duct-taped together with promises to be more tidy / spend more time together / get a joint cat.

When I came home from a weekend conference on digital information systems and found him moving the last few boxes of his stuff out of the house, I wasn't surprised.

"I need a cooling-off period," he said without looking at me.

The relationship was positively frigid already, though I didn't bring that up. I told myself it wouldn't have worked out regardless, and long before the diagnosis I'd been in denial that he was an asshole. My relationship wasn't the only one in support group to dissolve post-disease. We all had online dating stories, and debated when to tell people about the condition.

"Before the first date," I said.

"Before the first kiss," said Xavier.

"That's an asshole move," I said.

"Only one of my last five dates walked out the bar in a huff," he said. "The rest stayed long enough to drink their beer."

Of my last seven dates, five had canceled. Two had "something come up," one never got back to me, and two said I seemed really nice, but what would happen if we wanted to get intimate? I said that's why we used protection, but there was no changing their minds.

I told myself that if I didn't have the disease I would have been one of those open-minded people who were educated and unafraid. Tina and Robert had found each other in group and I was happy for that, though I was nervous to date another group member. Two weeks ago Xavier had walked me home from the meeting and come in for a drink and we'd made out on the couch, but afterward we sat holding hands and being scared.

"We're adults," he said. "If it didn't work out between us we could still be friends."

"It worked out for Tina and Robert," I said.

He kissed me when he left, but he hadn't called since then and hadn't been at the last group meeting. I should have called him, but hadn't yet.

Drive-throughs at donut places are great. You can order two cream-filled long johns with chocolate frosting, two rasp-berry-filled donuts, and two cinnamon rolls, and the donut-mak-ers put them in a bag and hand the bag out the drive-through window and you don't even have to worry about your hostage escaping. Then you can park your car and enjoy two donuts while continuing to inform and interrogate the hostage.

"I work from home," I told him. "Doing health insurance paperwork for a family practice doctor's office. I worked there as a nurse for seven years." Until I had to tell them I'd been diagnosed with the disease, and later found the shoebox with all my personal belongings at the front desk. Someone had already packed them up for me.

"When are we going to the station?"

"I lost my dad a couple of years ago to a stroke. Mom's still taking it hard. I bet your mom is going through the same kind of grieving process, and—"

"Lady," he said, "can you cut the bullshit and take me to the police station?"

I wiped my mouth on a napkin. "Listen, asshole. You interrupted my morning and my life, so we're going to follow my schedule. We'll get to the police station when I damn well please."

He crossed his arms, huddling into himself like a pouting child. I wanted to ask him about his pets, his siblings, stories about working with his dad at the repair shop and things he'd learned over those years, but he'd already shut down.

I'd seen that body language when I was a nurse and my patient didn't want to know more about her condition, or knew she wouldn't change the habits I was telling her to change. I'd seen that body language after I got the disease and had to tell people about it, and even other nurses leaned away slightly.

That was the case when I arrived at the police station, unlocked the passenger door, and ordered my hostage out of the car and through the swinging glass doors. I handed the plastic-wrapped knife to an officer, and dictated a statement about what had happened, then proofread his scrawl.

"We'll call if we need other information before the trial," the officer said, giving me a polite nod and a smile in lieu of a handshake. I'm sure my hostage would demand a scalding shower and perhaps a bleach bath and that all of his clothing be destroyed.

But I had four more donuts in the takeout bag, so I could go home, change out of my nightgown, continue my day, and know that I'd have a real story for support group next time. Everyone would nod and grimace and laugh, then we'd eat cookies, share hugs, and maybe Xavier would walk home with me again, holding hands this time, and I'd invite him inside for a longer visit.

You May Mistake This for a Love Story

HIS SMALL OFFICE is attached to the main one but the door is often closed, so I see him mostly at the copy machine. We make jokes about our cats. We both like cats.

This is a good sign, the first one. There will be more, and then we will date, and get engaged, and be married for nineteen years, and then we will get a divorce, mostly amicable, no law-yers, just threats of hiring them, a civility similar to the end of my first marriage.

I am taking notes on what will be our relationship, writing them on a pad at my desk in shorthand since no one else in the office can read it, and because I want to test my vision. I can see everything quite clearly, but my memory isn't as good as my sight. Thus the notes.

THIS IS WHAT people used to believe: when you were deprived of one sense, the others would become keener. That was the world of a too-cruel and too-just god (don't think too deeply about it), one who'd smite you in a second or gift you with extraordinary abilities. My right eye has been blind since birth, so it has been blessed for an equally long period of time. It is the eye that Dalí would have loved. Malleable. Mutable. It can see anything but mostly the future, an invisible stick-on eye in the middle of my back, my forehead, my knee, under my left breast, over my heart. It is where it needs to be. While my left eye must squint to read the fine print, the right sees at a glance that the kid asking for a late pass was making out with his girlfriend in the back of his mom's car during second period. Eye omnipotent. I give him the pass. Sometimes I am kind, even to liars. My right eye sees what it should and what it should not, playing on a separate screen in my mind. Actually it isn't like that exactly, but the analogy might help you understand.

HE'S THE ASSISTANT athletic director at the high school, almost like the assistant principal in that he works on schedules, charts grades, and yells at members of the football/basketball/wrestling team if they're failing classes. I'm the administrative assistant, meaning I answer the phone, soothe irate parents, write hall passes, separate the honestly tardy from those who were smoking under the bleachers between classes, and generally serve as all-knowing oracle and keeper of institutional information. In the future people will find it funny that he and I fell in love, but it is the classic myth. Jock dates nerd girl. Apollo chasing Cassandra. Think about it a moment and you'll see it's obvious.

MY EYE ALLOWS me to see love like a landscape. I take notes when no one is needfully standing beside my desk. The librarian will have an affair with the biology teacher—nice fellow, no kids, broke up with longtime girlfriend two and a half years ago, does laundry on Saturdays, doesn't wear too much aftershave, makes good stir-fry. The affair will last six months, just dinner and movies and sex at his apartment, then he'll move to a different school district in another state because the job pays more. They will both mourn. She'll feel betrayed but shoved by invisible hands to go to marriage counseling. Her husband will never know what happened. She'll think of him as sweet and oblivious. He'll wonder why she's suddenly more creative in the bedroom. (My eye squints to give them privacy.) This is as happy an ending as anyone can expect, and better than most.

YOU'D SAY I'M a liar and I am, but listen to this: I knew I would marry my first husband then divorce him fourteen years, eight months, and six days later, a month before I turned thirty-nine. All our friends thought the split was too amicable, which may or may not have been true, but they hadn't seen what I had, the slow replacement of our cells over time, the crinkles at the sides of our eyes at different jokes, the changing tilt of our heads when we'd nod at each other after work, the shifting weight of a kiss on the lips, how it slid over months to a kiss on the cheek.

PEOPLE SHAPE YOU. You shape people. This is part of love. Because of my first husband I eat a peppermint when I'm feeling stressed, make eye contact when I say hello, and know the biographies of three comic book superheroes. Because of me he makes lists, doesn't feel offended when a woman holds the door, and knows the lyrics to eighties pop songs. There are words/images/notes we can't read/see/hear without thinking of each other. Everyone is an unwitting Pygmalion and a block of marble, the chisel and the shaking hand.

THIS WILL BE the story of my third date with the athletic director: Going out for pizza, we both try to pay. He wants to be traditional. I have money, dammit, and he paid for the first two dates. We decide to take turns. This agreement will lounge in a corner of our minds even when we are married, even when we divorce. He cooks, I do dishes. He cleans the bathroom, I vacuum the cat hair (and cat hair and cat hair). We alternate weeks for grocery shopping. It is our slavish attention to the illusion of fairness, the cooperation we strive for and almost never achieve, perfecting the drive for perfection.

MY EYE, AN unwilling voyeur, stuck to the back of my elbow in the lunch line when I buy bottled water and a turkey sandwich, seeing the high school cafeteria in all its beauty and drama, gossip hanging in the air like violet clouds. Remember, Romeo and Juliet were teenagers. Nobody understands that better than someone who works with high school students.

Yes, sometimes I want to rest my eye, close it, stick it in a mug with my pens, but it's always open. I wish I could be like the Graeae—you probably don't remember them so I'll explain the story, how those three gray sisters shared one tooth and eye and fought over them constantly in a small dank cave where I doubt there was much of anything to see.

But what a blessing, I think, to be occasionally blank, devoid of visions.

THIS IS ANOTHER myth few people know, how Medusa was a beautiful woman who made love to Poseidon in Athena's temple. The goddess was pissed—you never know what people will do when you're not home—so she changed Medusa into the snake-haired woman who turned soldiers to statues. Sad, I think, how we focus only on the end of the story, skip the part about making love and go directly to stone. How like and unlike humans.

HE HAD TWO girlfriends before me, serious ones, neither of whom he wanted to marry. He will tell me about them on the fourth date when we are still in the auditioning phase, and I am no longer a paper-thin persona from the office, but a collage of memories and expressions and habits, someone he could care about. This is the period of sweetness and tenuousness. This is not love. It is antsy and easy and mostly performance. It comes with the process. Remember this: Love can have a steely or rusted or porous surface, or glint so bright you shouldn't look directly at it. Wait five minutes and love will change.

THIS IS ONE of our best evenings together: a long walk around the park across from his house, which became our house when we married four years and two months ago. We stroll past the men who always stand on the shore of the pond, ostensibly fishing but content to never catch anything. The intention matters most.

We hold hands and he walks on my left. He has known to be on my left since the second date. That is one of the reasons why I knew he was a keeper. We don't talk much, just a few words about spreadsheets—their endless tyranny, his eyestrain due to the small print. I say maybe he needs a new prescription. He does not like the idea of stronger glasses. I shrug. A lens is a lens is a lens. He rests his arm around my shoulders to say maybe I am right. We keep walking. We will have thirteen more good years and two mediocre ones before the divorce, when he talks of retiring to upstate New York where he grew up. Too cold, I say, but this is where my farsightedness is lacking. I can't see how to avoid the split, find a different trajectory, another curve in the path. Perhaps this is the blessed curse of knowing the future—knowing you can't change it, settling with the inevitable, continuing to walk with that knowledge in still-comfortable silence.

YOU CAN'T TELL a sixteen-year-old that their sporadic rushes of emotions aren't love but hormones. You can't work against the tidal rise and fall of their voices in the guidance counselor's office. Like the sea, that kind of surge isn't meant to be contained. I watch the daily storms while standing in the cafeteria line—the swells of pink affection, the steely gray crash of breakups, the soothing blue words of friends who try to comfort the bereaved, though it never works. Everyone wants to paddle out to the next wave. Like anyone who chooses to live by the sea, I am accustomed to the noise. Love isn't always crashing waves, there are calm places, lakes that are placid and not wind-whipped, where a boat could sail for hours undisturbed, but not everyone wants that sort of affection. More exciting, especially when you are young, to have the kind of lust that hits you in the face, leaves you near-drowning in the rush of being alive. Often life is best realized when it is edged with death, or at least the illusion that one might be dying. While there are all kinds of love-scapes, my eye, unblinking, has no preference. It is not a matter of taste, but change that must be embraced.

PEOPLE CHANGE. RELATIONSHIPS change. They are like the ocean, never still, an idea that scares too many of us. Most want to believe in till death do us part, that they can ride on the crest of waves and ignore the depth of the sea, a large and obvious detail. I never mention this tenuousness to lovers, though my reasoning is silly. I fear no one would love me if I couldn't say I'd love them forever, as if a love that won't last isn't worth having in the first place.

"I'll love you forever," my ex-husband said the day after we married.

No, I wanted to say, *you'll love me for fourteen years, eight months, and six days, and then you won't stop loving me, but you'll love me in a way that means we shouldn't be married anymore, which is fine, which is the nature of love. It changes, it grows, it swells and condenses and divides.*

Instead I said, "I love you too," and I did.

I'm not saying love isn't real. I'm saying it's alive.

Costume Control

IT WASN'T ILLEGAL to sell brand-name magical clothing, but purchasing it was prohibitively expensive for most people. That explained the burgeoning black market and rise in the number of imitations. As Deputy General of Costuming Enforcement, I did what I could to educate the public, but buying a knockoff could have disastrous consequences. There were the explosions, the spontaneous lizards, and, as was common with magical cloaks, the reappearance of the entire body except for one hand. Most of the time the hand was still there, the person in question just needed to wear a glove to make that apparent.

"I spent a week's wages on that dress!" a lady yelled at me when my assistant Melinda and I confiscated a dark blue ball gown that was supposed to grant its wearer eternal youth. She was not swayed when I explained that some buyers had accelerated their pace of aging when they took the dress off, while others got a nasty toe fungus.

"Let me worry about that," she said, but of course she wouldn't worry about that, so Melinda had to restrain her while I zipped the dress in a plastic bag and took it out to our SUV. There were too many fly-by-night companies producing garments that didn't come with a certificate of authenticity or proper training for its use, something that was required with more sophisticated cloaks, dresses, and time-travel watches. Items like those might require weeks of lessons, multi-volume owners' guides, release forms, and specific insurance policies. Contrary to the whispers of black marketeers, we weren't saying that working-class people couldn't own such clothing. They simply couldn't afford safe models, so it was better that they not have such clothing at all.

"You'll take that hat over my dead body," one lady screeched as we nestled a black beret in a metal box. Her long hair barely concealed the third ear that had sprouted on one side of her neck, but those snafus weren't my department.

"Maybe she would have stopped at the fifth ear," I said to Melinda as we got back into the SUV. My assistant shook her head. None of us in the agency understood why so few people appreciated our protective mission. If their neighbor's time-travel watch exploded and took five other houses with it, then they'd be crying for our help. It was far easier to collect all the contraband and incinerate it, aside from the few items we could authenticate as being from reputable manufacturers. Those were sold at auction to fund our operations.

Most of my critics would have been hiding under their desks after the first day, even if they were wearing my standard accessories, including the anti-incantation necklace, bracelet, and underwear, which I only employed for cases that seemed particularly volatile.

I relished the order-restoring nature of my work, which was far different from trying to raise a thirteen-year-old girl. I knew thirteen-year-olds were natural rebels, but when I joined the agency I hoped that Jenna would wear the amulet I'd bought to help her eyesight. She was blind in one eye due to complications from a premature birth, and nearsighted due to heredity, so I worried about who or what she wouldn't see when crossing the street.

"It gives me a headache," she said when I asked why she didn't have it on, "and the vision in my blind eye is so fuzzy it's distracting."

"The headache would stop and your sight would improve if you wore the pendant more often. Don't you want to be able to see better?"

"I guess," she said in a tone that implied the opposite.

"Just put it aside until she gets older," said her father, who lived in Seattle and coordinated health inspections for low-income apartments. He'd moved there after the divorce, and he and Jenna spoke frequently on the phone. My ex and I were amicable when we had time to talk, which wasn't often, so it wasn't that different from the way things had been when we were married.

"Why can't my amulet go to someone who needs it?" Jenna asked at dinner.

"Honey," I said, "do we have to talk about this now?"

"I don't want it," she said. "There are lots of kids in children's hospitals who might."

"I know that, honey," I said, "but perhaps you could save up your babysitting money and buy another amulet for one of them."

"Dad doesn't have a whole suit that costs as much as your amulet or earrings or bracelet or cloak," she said.

I took a deep breath. "I need them to do my job."

"We don't need the traveling shoes," she said.

"You enjoyed the trip to Japan."

Jenna crossed her arms and pouted. My ex had made a few pointed comments about my clothing budget, but I reminded him that he worked in domestic affairs while I was involved in more delicate operations.

"I bought the amulet for your safety," I said.

Jenna stared at her potatoes.

Understand that when you had a child with an impairment like Jenna's, you worried all the time about things she couldn't see—buses when crossing the street, people she bumped into at the grocery store, basketballs headed in her direction during gym class. And when you had a position like mine, people wondered if you were a skinflint, walking around with a bona fide magic cloak while your child slammed into a skateboarder and chipped her front tooth because she didn't know to get out of the way.

No one said anything about Jenna to me directly, but I could see the questions in their eyes. Blindness. Deafness. Speech impediments. Those had been some of the easiest things to cure with early amulets, and you didn't need an instruction manual. Sometimes there were side effects like headaches, but they disappeared as you became accustomed to the amulet and it became accustomed to you.

But forcing the amulet into my daughter's hands was more difficult than prying (faux) magical clothing out of the hands of others.

THE PROBLEM STARTED three days later when I searched for my traveling shoes. I felt like a beach vacation was in order. Jenna could sit on the sand and pout if she wished, but I needed a few palm trees, a good book, and a fruity iced drink that contained alcohol. Maybe if we spent a day or two there, she would consent to having a nice good time. I couldn't find the shoes I wanted in my closet, a pair that looked like sandals, but I had three sets (to match different outfits and occasions) and I didn't always put them back in an orderly fashion.

"We haven't taken a vacation in a while," I said to Jenna at breakfast, "and I thought we could go to the beach this weekend."

"I have homework," she said without looking up from the book she was currently reading. "And a group project that's due on Monday."

"We'll get away on Saturday," I said. "Just for the afternoon and dinner, then come back that evening."

"Whatever," she said.

I ate my toast, drank my espresso, and figured I'd resume the search for the traveling sandals when I got home. I'd peered under my bed and in various cabinets, since even the best traveling shoes occasionally decided to take a jaunt on their own.

Once they had climbed to the top of the refrigerator, and another time I found them on a bookshelf, so I figured I had to be patient.

I didn't expect to find them while Melinda and I searched the closet of a bank teller on the north side of town. We'd heard she had a mind-reading bracelet, and after we found that, we had to inspect her closet as well. Standard protocol. My traveling sandals were there, the sequined straps unmistakable.

"Where did you get these?" I said, turning to the woman who was sitting cross-armed on her bed.

She snorted. "I have the certificate."

"Show me," I said. She took it from a locked box beside her jewelry box. There was a coffee stain in the corner of the certificate that I knew too well, since I'd been angry at myself for leaving it on the kitchen table and vulnerable to breakfast stains.

"I have reason to believe these are stolen goods," I said.

"I bought them fair and square," she said.

It took ten more minutes, and a threat of driving her to the office for further questioning, before she admitted that she'd bought the shoes from a girl at her coffee shop last week. She was selling magical clothing and said she'd give the money to a food pantry.

"And you assumed it wasn't stolen merchandise?" I stuffed the shoes into a metal box.

The woman shrugged. "What do you call it when you have your little magical clothing auctions for rich people?"

"Legitimate," I said. I went home during my lunch hour, conducted a closet inventory, and reviewed the contents of my jewelry box to see what Jenna had taken. She hadn't touched the jewelry and underwear I needed for work, but she'd taken the earrings I wore to detect lying, the belt that let me breathe underwater, the amulet that allowed me to manifest objects smaller than a foot in diameter, and the traveling sandals.

I poked through Jenna's closet, and couldn't find her traveling shoes or the amulet in her jewelry box. Melinda and I had been planning two investigations that afternoon, but I was too rattled. Back at the office, the best I could do was sign paper-work.

I dropped the traveling sandals on the kitchen floor when I returned home. They tapped their heels together twice, asking where I wanted to go. Jenna sat at the kitchen table with an open textbook.

"I've heard about your black market operations," I said.

She glanced at the shoes and returned to her book. That was not acceptable.

"Look at me," I said, grabbing her book from the table. "What do you have to say for yourself?"

"Nothing." She glared up at me. "You know what I did."

"It's theft," I said.

"Nothing worse than what you're doing."

"But these people are buying clothing that is potentially dangerous."

"Ours isn't," she said. "so why can't I sell it?"

"Your amulet, too?"

"To someone who wanted it," she said. "Someone who couldn't afford it otherwise."

"The black market is illegal. You could be sent to a juvenile detention facility."

"Yes," she said, a slight smile emerging at the corners of her mouth. I slid down in a chair and crossed my arms to mirror my daughter.

"Why don't you want to see?" I asked, my voice rising higher than I expected.

"I've gotten along fine for thirteen years like this," she said. "This lady I met, she just lost her vision in one eye. It was a work accident. She should have been wearing goggles."

"That's her concern," I said. "I don't want another skate-boarder slamming into you because he's not looking where he's going."

"You can't stop every accident."

"I just want to help you," I said.

"Why can't you be okay with me? Dad is."

"That still doesn't justify stealing," I said.

"I'm trying to sell this stuff for a reasonable price," she said. "Why can't you fight for that, instead of running around taking shit from people? If magical clothing were cheaper, then the knockoff companies would go out of business."

"It isn't that easy," I said. "I can't control the economy."

"I'm not the only one stealing shit," she said under her breath.

I shoved my chair back from the table. My daughter was determined to be one of the renegades. But she had to be punished somehow. Everyone in the office would know about Jenna tomorrow, since we had to report black market activity. I paced my bedroom for twenty minutes before deciding on a course of action, one I had to take though I didn't want to.

"Pack your suitcase," I said when I went back downstairs. "Unless you promise to stop these thefts and apologize."

Jenna smirked at me, thinking she'd won and was going to a juvenile detention center. I had to be a responsible parent, dole out tough love, and be prepared to repeat that on national television. I asked Melinda to pick us up. I didn't know what else to do with my kid. I loved her. I was exasperated with her. And not a little embarrassed.

Jenna knitted her eyebrows when we pulled into the hospital parking lot, drove to the emergency room door, and I told her to get out.

"What are you doing?" she said.

"Honey," I said, "you need a psychological evaluation." And maybe a prolonged stay.

"There's nothing wrong with me," she said. "You can't do this."

But Melinda and I could do this, dragging her out of the car and through the doors as she howled and fought and then gave up, huddling in a plastic chair and curling into her impenetrable self. I would rather be called harsh than lenient, because I had to take care of my kid and deal with public opinion, and part of me hoped that a psychologist could explain why my child would refuse to wear a perfectly good amulet.

The news networks had pounced on the story by the next afternoon, fabricating rumors that my daughter had refused to eat solid food and needed to be fed intravenously, but Jenna had only been in the hospital for twenty-four hours.

"She's very intelligent," said the psychologist who called me that afternoon, "and determined to maintain her beliefs."

I stayed in the office all day, fielding calls and arranging interviews because I knew I couldn't fend them off. It was better to answer my detractors early, explain my rationale as a parent, and prove I had nothing to hide.

"It is an excellent facility," I said multiple times, "and she is receiving the best care."

I knew my daughter would lecture other patients about the need for price controls on magical clothing. She had her father's humanitarian genes, but he would frown on theft. Still, I knew I'd spend a week defending my parenting principles on national television, and waiting for some other government official to create a news event. I knew I wasn't that interesting.

My ex texted that evening to say he'd seen me on TV and supported my actions.

I know there probably wasn't time to call and consult me, he wrote, reminding me of the sideways conversations we'd had when still married. *We can't be raising a little delinquent.* Always the measured diplomat, even when we divorced. We didn't need to hire attorneys because he didn't care about the things I wanted, such as the house and car and furniture.

Every day after work I called the hospital to ask if Jenna wanted to talk with me. The answer was no. I wouldn't force myself on her, so I told the nurses to tell Jenna that I missed her, then I turned on the TV.

Her psychologist phoned me in the mornings, said Jenna was fine and keeping up with the homework her teachers sent. I wondered if she was happier in the hospital than with me. People had more time to spend with her there. That was their job. My job was preventing people from blowing themselves up, and/or growing unnecessary appendages.

Melinda was kind enough to invite me to her place for dinner.

"Any time you want to come over is fine," she said.

"I'm okay," I said, "but maybe later in the week."

After a week I stopped by the hospital to ask for the umpteenth time if Jenna wanted to talk with me. The nurse on duty checked as I waited in the reception area and watched sniffling, crying, snotty children burrow into their mothers' laps. For a moment I missed those sweet, disgusting years, ones filled with bad odors and bodily fluids. That was the time when kids were trusting and dependent and knew to take your hand in a vise grip when crossing the street.

The nurse returned, shaking her head. I nodded and drove home, telling myself it was good to savor a meal without trying to make a political point. My story had evaporated from the evening news, but that didn't explain why I was uptight and having problems sleeping. Everyone in the office agreed I was handling the attention well. I was media savvy, cool as the proverbial cucumber, which didn't explain why I felt like checking myself in for a mental evaluation.

I thought about having Melinda over for dinner, which would give me a chance to wonder aloud if I'd really needed to put Jenna in the hospital, but I could guess her answer.

"You didn't have a choice," she'd say, because I didn't have a choice and because she was working under me. But I wanted someone else to come up with an option I hadn't considered.

Because I wanted to use my traveling shoes, and was a bit too much in need of company, I texted my ex and asked if I could meet him after work for a drink. He was three time zones behind me, and said that would be fine.

"Jenna is doing okay," I said, swirling the wine in my glass. He knew my tastes and had chosen a nice bar.

"I know," he said. "I spoke with her today."

"You did?" I said, trying to keep my voice light.

"Mondays, Wednesdays, Fridays, and Saturdays," he said. "Our usual schedule."

"Of course," I said, though I hadn't realized that was the case.

"She's doing a lot of thinking," he said and paused. "And a lot of reading."

"That's what I figured," I said.

"Stealing is wrong," he said, his voice now slower and more tired. "There are other ways to make a point."

"I know," I said, wondering if there was anything else I should ask him, but I was blank. We made small talk—his job, my job, the annoyance of perennial funding shortages—-then I finished the last sip of wine, told him to have a good evening, and we'd talk again later. He returned my nod, then I disappeared from the bar to the beach where I'd wanted to go with Jenna.

I arrived at sunset, removed my sandals, and strolled for a while in the sand. I wanted to be soothed by the sound of waves, but still felt tension in my shoulders. With all her free time and extra books, Jenna would return to me more of a rebel than when she'd left. I fretted all weekend, then returned to Seattle on Monday evening, hoping my ex would have time to talk.

"I don't know what to do," I said, trying not to sound as helpless as I felt and hoping the wine would steady me.

"Well," he said, speaking more to his gin and tonic than to me, "perhaps she could live with me for a while. I know a couple of good schools here that she'd probably like."

"And you have enough space in your apartment?"

"Her room is always ready."

I knew she'd be fine. Better than fine. She'd be happy.

"Call her," I said, then downed the rest of the glass. "You probably already talked about travel arrangements and changing the custody arrangement. We'll be in touch."

I set my glass on the table and nodded my goodbye. I shouldn't have been so curt, but couldn't stand the sight of him at that moment, or how pleased Jenna would be with a new school in a new town where she could continue her crusade and I wouldn't hear about it. A day later, Jenna called to say what I should pack in her suitcase.

"Dad is going to send me to an international school," she said. "Think about all the other kids I'll meet, and the stuff I can learn about where they're from, and—"

"Sounds great," I said, folding her clothes and wondering if I should keep the house. Maybe I needed to streamline, find a smaller place with smaller closets. This would be best for everyone concerned. It didn't mean I was a bad mother. I'd raised her for four years and I suppose it was fair for him to have the next five.

I drove Jenna's bags to the hospital. She'd leave in the morning, and I told the nurses I'd return to give her a hug goodbye. They said she was very excited. I took Melinda up on her invitation for dinner. I liked her mellow husband and two kids, daughters who wore bracelets against enchantments, since Melinda said you couldn't be too careful. Dinner was very good—Melinda's husband made a great lasagna—and her girls chattered about school and recess and how they didn't have much homework. When I excused myself to use the bathroom, I could still hear them laughing in the kitchen. It was too much. I knew what I did next was terribly rude, but my kid was leaving the next day and Melinda would understand my early departure. I'd worn my traveling shoes to her house, so it was simple to pop into the fourth-floor ladies' room at the hospital. I didn't want it to look too strange when I walked out to the nurses' station and asked to see my daughter.

She was in the activity room with a bunch of little kids who were wearing bright pajamas. The television was showing cartoons, some kids played with blocks, and my daughter had a girl perched on her lap and was reading a story. Her eyes narrowed when she saw me, then she finished the book and slid the girl off her lap while two other kids begged for another.

"In a moment," she said, "but someone else gets to choose. I have to speak with this lady."

"Who's called your mother," I said.

My daughter strode past me and into the hall. I had to follow.

"Why are you here?" She crossed her arms. The sweet babysitter had evaporated. This was my usual kid.

"I packed all the clothes you wanted. You could thank me."

"Thanks. I thought you were going to come back in the morning."

"I wanted more than five minutes. I wanted to talk."

"What else do you have to say?"

I paused. I wasn't sure. I loved her? I would miss her? Did I need to say that? Didn't she know?

"Let me know when you figure it out," she said, opening the playroom door. "We don't have much longer for story time before they have to go to bed."

I doubt she expected me to follow her, but I did. I took off my shoes and put them on a high shelf where the little ones couldn't reach them. All I'd ever wanted was for my child to be safe and healthy, and I wasn't leaving until she believed it. But now there were the kids, and they wanted this story and that story, and they were swarming my daughter and waving books. One little boy, a short kid who was in the back of the crowd, changed tactics and walked over to me with his book. Another adult. Another reader. I said okay. Just one. My daughter was occupied anyway.

I sat on a beanbag chair and the kid climbed on my lap and I didn't mind his hair in my face. Jenna's hair always did that. I started reading, and did voices for the different characters like I did when my kid was little, since dragons sounded different from princesses, who sounded different from witches. Two and then three more kids clustered around by the time I was halfway through, and Jenna's book must have been short because she'd stopped reading, so the rest of the kids came over, too.

I glanced up to see my daughter in profile, which was a bit better than when she had her head down. I finished the first book, but one girl waved another at me. I said okay, just one more, but it must be getting close to their bedtime. I glanced to the shelf. My shoes were still there. I glanced to my daughter, her head tilted slightly away from me, but she turned back when I opened the book and started reading again. The ex always said I was the better storyteller. I wondered if, tomorrow, my daughter might tell him this story. I chose to think she might. I kept reading.

Acknowledgments and Gifts

Seven gallons of mint chocolate chip ice cream to Tristan, in thanks for being my editor and perennial partner in crime who reads all first drafts and has helped many of these stories find their final form.

A kangaroo finger puppet to my mother, for encouraging my sense of play, singing with me in grocery store aisles, and understanding that the steering wheel can be used as a percussion instrument when sitting at red lights.

A mountain of chocolate chip peanut butter cookies to Trudy Lewis, Phong Nyugen, and the members of my workshop groups at the University of Missouri. Thank you for reading early drafts of several of these stories, offering kind and constructive comments, and knowing the right places to laugh.

A lifetime supply of sticky notes, two boxes of their favorite pens, and my sincere gratitude to the editors of literary magazines where several of these stories were originally published.

"White as Soap," "Switching Heads," and "Sisyphus" first appeared in *Pleiades*; "Athena," and "Feet" first appeared in *PANK*; "Marbles" first appeared in *Andromeda Spaceways Magazine*; "Berchta," "The Dreamlords," and "In the Dim Below" first appeared in *Guernica*; "The Mirror" first appeared in *The Female Complaint:*

Tales of Unruly Women; "The Pieces" first appeared in *Strange Horizons*; "The Hero" first appeared in *Indiana Review*; "Sphinx" first appeared in *Kugelmass*; and "You May Mistake This for a Love Story" first appeared in *Pembroke Magazine*.

About the Author

Teresa Milbrodt grew up in Bowling Green, Ohio, which is not a bad place to be even though it is a former swamp. She received her M.F.A. from Bowling Green State University and her Ph.D. from the University of Missouri, and has taught English and creative writing classes for several years. She is the author of two short story collections, *Bearded Women* and *Work Opportunities*; a novel, *The Patron Saint of Unattractive People*; and a flash fiction collection, *Larissa Takes Flight*. She believes in coffee, long walks, face-to-face conversation, and writing the occasional haiku.

Also from Shade Mountain Press

NOVELS

Stephanie Allen, *Tonic and Balm*
In 1919 a traveling medicine show, featuring both black and white performers, reels in rural audiences with variety acts and patent-medicine flimflam. Great Groups Reads pick, 2019.

Kirsten Imani Kasai, *The House of Erzulie*
A tale of obsession and racial guilt on an 1850s Louisiana plantation. Editors' Choice, *Historical Novels Review*. "A propulsive read"—*Booklist*.

Vanessa Garcia, *White Light*
A young Cuban-American artist distills her grief, rage, and love onto the canvas. Praised by Nobel laureate Wole Soyinka for its "lyrical pace and texture." An NPR Best Book of 2015.

Yi Shun Lai, *Not a Self-Help Book: The Misadventures of Marty Wu*
Marty Wu, compulsive reader of advice manuals, ricochets between a stressful job in New York and the warmth of extended family in Taiwan. Semi-finalist, 2017 Thurber Prize for American Humor.

Lynn Kanter, *Her Own Vietnam*
Decades after serving as a U.S. Army nurse in Vietnam, a woman confronts buried wartime memories and unresolved family issues. Silver Award, Foreword INDIES Book of the Year.

SHORT STORY COLLECTIONS

Robin Parks, *Egg Heaven*
Lyrical tales of diner waitresses and their customers, living the un-glamorous life in Southern California. Hailed by *Kenyon Review* as a "welcome addition" to working-class fiction.

***The Female Complaint: Tales of Unruly Women,*
   edited by Rosalie Morales Kearns**
Short story anthology featuring nonconformists, troublemakers, and other indomitable women. Finalist, Foreword INDIES Book of the Year.

POETRY

Mary A. Hood, *All the Spectral Fractures*
New and collected poems by the microbiologist/naturalist/poet. "Spans a prolific career bridging the scientific with the lyric"—Jill McCabe Johnson.

All books are available at our website, www.ShadeMountainPress.com, as well as bookstores and online retailers.